The Perfect Arrangement

by

Susan Payne

This is a work of fiction. Names, characters, places, and incidents are either the product of the author's imagination or are used fictitiously, and any resemblance to actual persons living or dead, business establishments, events, or locales, is entirely coincidental.

The Perfect Arrangement

COPYRIGHT © 2022 by Susan Payne

Cover Art by *The Wild Rose Press, Inc.*

The Wild Rose Press, Inc.
PO Box 708
Adams Basin, NY 14410-0708
Visit us at www.thewildrosepress.com

Publishing History
First Edition, 2022
Trade Paperback ISBN 978-1-5092-4138-5
Digital ISBN 978-1-5092-4139-2

Published in the United States of America

Dedication

I dedicate this book to my family who are always there when I need them—and I always need them.

London 1815

CHAPTER ONE

Sarah moved through the silent house wondering if this was what the rest of her life would sound like. She had sent Aggie, her woman of all work, and Vernon, the man who took care of the yard and any maintenance needs, away for the rest of the day. The last of her husband's mourners were gone, as well, and now she finally had time to think.

Yesterday she only had time to react, not even feel. In fact, she could remember the numbness as it crawled through her body leaving her little more than a shell. She must have retained some semblance of normalcy or perhaps others were cognizant of the shock she was coping with. After all, she had said good-bye to her husband of two years in the morning and his body was brought into the house for the wake that afternoon.

She greeted the neighbors and people her husband knew and she did it with the same tranquil manner. Accepting their condolences, their memories of her husband as they knew him, their curious expressions wanting to know what had happened, but not crass enough to ask.

Not that Sarah could have answered their questions. The men who brought her husband to her did not have answers although they were very professional, very kind and careful they didn't nick any of the parlor furniture as they brought the polished wood casket in. She should be grateful that her husband's man of business was so thorough, so, well, business-like so that she hadn't needed to do anything. It had been all handled for her. That was the only thing she had to be thankful for—that, and the fact her husband hadn't seemed to have suffered at the end.

As she stood by the coffin earlier that day, before he had been taken to the small cemetery nearby, she tried to feel something, anything to justify all those people speaking so kindly to her. She couldn't. No matter how hard she dug through her memories. That wasn't to say she wouldn't miss her husband or wouldn't mourn him, but so far, no tears had fallen, no sleepless night. Maybe that would come later. Once the fact he was gone finally became a reality and not simply a day of people coming and going from her house, expressions of sympathy she hadn't felt she deserved, the kindness of strangers.

She moved slowly, dragging her feet up the stairs to her room—it used to be the room where her husband visited her each Wednesday, but now it belonged solely to her. Maybe there she would notice her loss, notice the absence of another living, breathing human being. The reflection in the mirror showed she was still human. Wearing one of her dresses dyed black the day before by Aggie whose first thought had been for mourning clothes. A black arm band wasn't going to be sufficient for a wife—a widow.

Aggie was good in that way. Thinking ahead and doing what needed to be done. Sarah never needed to worry about ordering Aggie about or Vernon, either, for that matter. Aggie ordered the poor man around as well as everyone else.

Taking the dress off, she hung it over the back of the chair. Climbing into bed, Sarah wondered when it would all hit her. When she would break down and howl at the moon for leaving her a widow at the age of two and twenty, having her start over when she thought her life settled, her life content if not exactly as she had expected it to be.

Staring at the ceiling, she was aware she hadn't thought about her husband. Hadn't asked herself why he was killed in a buggy accident outside of town when she thought him safe inside the law offices where he worked. Hadn't wondered what had gone through his mind as the buggy flipped and the horse whinnied in shock and pain, if he had had time to think of her before his neck had snapped. She thought about these things purposely to force herself to feel something. Anything. Instead, she felt her eyelids flutter close, and sleep overtook her mind.

Sarah woke to the sounds of Aggie in the kitchen and birds chirping in the tree outside the window. The same pair of robins nested there each spring and then continued to make it their night resting place along with whatever fledglings wishing to stay close to home. They always let her know when the sun's rays were beginning to light the eastern sky.

Redressing in black, she wrapped her hair easily around her hand and pinned it in place at the back of her head. Glancing quickly into the mirror, she washed her face and used the tooth powder she had ignored the night before. Everything seemed to take so long, take so much energy she simply wanted to get downstairs to normalcy. But what was going to be her new normal? This would have been the time she would have been helping her husband with his cravat, reminding him to take the papers from his desk, telling him what was planned for dinner that evening.

Finding Aggie still in the kitchen began to make the day feel more normal.

"Oh, Miss Sarah, I just finished sortin' the cups and flatware to return to the neighbors. I'll wait a bit and then when I'm sure they're awake, I'll run them back over."

"Be sure to thank them for me, won't you, Aggie? I don't know if I did so yesterday, but we did need them. I wasn't aware of all the people my husband knew." She went to the stove to find the kettle hot and poured the water into the teapot setting ready on the counter.

"You did that yesterday, but I'll make sure to tell them again. We here in Bloomsbury stick together through hard times. We ain't like them folks over in Mayfair."

"Well, if we lived in Mayfair, I doubt we would have had to borrow enough dishware to cover the number of mourners who came to the funeral." Getting out a cup she continued, "I want to thank you for finding an open-minded vicar to say words at the burial. Richard kept saying he was an atheist so I rather hope he won't haunt me for giving him a Christian funeral. After all, I couldn't really build a barge and set it on fire in the Thames." At her friend's confounded expression, she explained, "He read about how Vikings got rid of their dead and told me when he was old and gray to give him that kind of funeral. I might have done so if I had had more time to plan things."

Walking into the dining room she whispered to herself, "No one tells you how fast it all happens. What little time there is to plan anything besides the traditional…"

Continuing on, she found herself at her husband's office and sat at her husband's desk. It was neat with only the ink bottle and quills on the surface along with the blotting pad. She opened the drawer not knowing what she expected to find but hoped she would recognize anything that should be sent to her husband's office. The office where he was working toward making partner. He had been a first-rate barrister according to all who were aware of his work, all those men in expensive coats and breeches who came through the house examining everything as if they were appraising it for an estate sale.

Opening the middle drawer, she found the plain and letterheaded paper, sealing wax, pencils, quills, a small penknife to sharpen the quills, and envelopes. All neatly piled waiting for his use. The upper righthand drawer was locked so she chose the next one down and found the household accounts just as she knew they would be there. Although she kept the accounts, Richard always went over them before putting them away.

She remembered asking why he did that as if he didn't trust her. He told her it wasn't about trust, but that he wanted to know what was going on in his house. That he liked to know what was paid for a beef roast or length of lace. Perhaps that was all it was since he never chastised her for overspending on anything. As if she would. She and Aggie prided themselves in being thrifty and making the house budget stretch to include many more items than normal, including the new draperies in the parlor. Long trips to Cheapside and the warehouses there brought rewards that had made her home attractive without damaging the budget.

The bottom drawer held a bottle of whiskey, opened with two empty glasses. She picked them up and smelled them. They had definitely been used, and she wondered when the last time her husband felt the need to have a drink? Was it to celebrate a win or smooth over a loss? No one ever visited him at his home office, it was simply where he would disappear to in the evenings. Perhaps to do no more than have a quiet drink alone.

She peered quizzically at the still locked drawer and then remembered the small packet of items given to her by the undertaker. She went to the front entrance and pulled open the drawer that normally held gloves. She found what she had been searching for on top and returned to the desk. As she emptied the items from her hand, a coin rolled over the edge of the desk and onto the carpet. She ignored it as she avidly searched for a key.

There it was. A small key she didn't recognize, certainly not her house key. When she tried it, found it was too large for the drawer. She fingered through the other items, but other than his usual fob of house and office keys, a clean handkerchief, a few more coins, and silver toothpick holder there wasn't anything of notice. She left them there. She didn't know what to do with his things, items he had taken out nightly and placed on a dish in his room only to place them back into his pocket the next morning.

The door knocker sounded, and she hurried to answer hoping it wasn't someone who couldn't make the funeral, but wished to give their condolences. She was done hearing about death, thinking about death knowing the scent of roses would forever remind her of yesterday. Opening the door, she found a young boy in livery holding out an envelope.

"For Mrs. Richard Harris."

She accepted the missive and the boy turned quickly walking back to the street without waiting for a vail. She stood staring at the neat script and the name of her husband's law-firm before realizing she should close the door. Tearing open the envelope, she found a brief note from her husband's man of business who worked at the same firm. She knew that, of course, but the note stated she was to ask to see her husband's employer. One of the named attorneys at the firm, the one who was grooming her husband to become a barrister in London, although it would have taken years before Richard would have been given any major cases. So far, he had worked mostly with penny-ante criminals and crimes. He had told her the best would come later. Then he would be able to ask whatever fees he wanted from the gentry and aristocracy who needed his expertise.

Noting the man asked for a meeting as soon as was feasibly possible, Sarah checked the clock on the mantel and found she could easily make an early afternoon appointment. Feeling at loose ends, she went to tell Aggie she was going out and not to bother with making a dinner, that she would find something for herself later.

Sitting in the waiting room of the austere offices where her husband spent most of his waking hours, she peered discreetly around trying not to appear like a country bumpkin in town for the first time. The dark wainscoting appeared to be throughout the rooms and even continued down the halls toward the private offices. She knew Richard had had one of those offices, but had never been invited to visit him, and she had never invaded him at work when she was out shopping.

He always seemed to want his work and his home

life kept separate, never bringing associates or friends home for dinner or a game of chess. That was what his club was for he had informed her when she offered to be his hostess if he ever decided to hold a dinner or gathering. Instead, the first time she met any of them it was while standing beside her husband's coffin.

"Mrs. Harris? Sir William will see you now if you care to follow me."

She was shaken out of her reverie and followed the polite young man. Had he been at the funeral yesterday? She couldn't say for sure so decided it was best not to say anything. He knew she was newly widowed since she had received the same sort of 'look' from everyone she had met so far. Some met her gaze and smiled slightly while others glanced away quickly without making full eye-contact. That was all right with her. She didn't know what to say, either.

A robust, older man stood as she entered another darkly paneled room and said, rather heartily, "Mrs. Harris, I'm sorry to have been out of town yesterday and miss the funeral. So sad for us to meet under such difficult times." He ushered her into one of the two chairs in front of his desk and then returned to his own. "Could I order you some tea?"

"No, thank you, Sir William." Anxious to get this meeting over with, to know how poorly she was now financially situated, she brought up the subject on both their minds. "I take it this is about my husband's will?"

"Ah, a no-nonsense sort of woman. I would expect no less from Richard's wife." He pulled some sheaves of paper toward him. "Let's get right to it. As you must know, there isn't much to the estate. An account at the Royal Bank of Scotland, a small bond bought on a canal which was never started so we shall consider it worthless, and your home on Curzon Street."

"My what?" Sarah thought the man had misspoken. That address was in Mayfair, and Richard had explained more than once they could not afford such a luxurious address.

"I said, your home at Number 9, Curzon Street. The deed shall be signed over to you since you have no male relative to control your property. I expect you will keep on Mr. Winters, your husband's man of business? He will help with budgeting and making sure taxes are paid."

She was flummoxed, but didn't want to show her shock to a stranger for the third day in a row and merely nodded, unsure if she would be able to afford the man after hearing what she had been bequeathed. She knew the balance of their bank account, and it wasn't more than a month or two of household expenses what with the rent and cost for fire protection which was mandatory under their rental contract. Without it, if their house caught fire, no one would attempt to put it out and if anyone arrived would only protect those surrounding buildings that had been insured.

"I guess you were correct when you said this shouldn't take long. I knew there wasn't much as Richard was only starting out and all. I appreciate you taking the time to speak with me, personally, Sir William." She gathered her reticule and readied to stand.

"Well, I had high hopes for your husband. A fine mind and a fine man. He could have gone far, perhaps even become a judge. A da…I mean, a sad shame his life ended so soon."

"Thank you for the praise. He thought very highly

of you, also." Unable to voice the question upper most in her mind, she stood as he did. "I'll leave you to get on with your other clients. I searched for any papers to do with his work in his office at home, but found nothing."

"Winters checked your husband's desk here for any personal items and placed them in a box to be sent to your home. In fact, they may already be there by the time you return." He remained standing as she shook his hand before being escorted to the door.

All the way home in the hackney, Sarah kept thinking back to the house on Curzon in the expensive Mayfair area. Could it have been meant as a surprise? Possibly for their anniversary that was coming up? Her husband knew she had dreamed of living there and had felt their address was the main reason Richard never wanted to entertain or bring his friends home. Although it was a lovely house and she had made it more than comfortable, the area was no longer popular. He probably thought it would make the other members of the law firm look down on him. This Curzon address, on the other hand, was perfect.

She hurried into the house and went directly to the office to find the unknown key. Picking it up, she examined its size and realized it could fit a door lock. She had the key to the home Richard had bought for them. Too late to enjoy it together, but it meant her small amount of funds would stretch further, possibly to half a year if she was frugal.

It was too late today to travel out again that day, but first thing in the morning she would take the key and investigate her new home. She would keep it a secret until she unveiled it as a *fait accompli* for Aggie. After all, it may need some renovations before they could move in. She could sew draperies as she had for the parlor here, and Vernon was more than able to paint and fix anything around a house. Excitement bubbled up as she wished she could have enjoyed this with the man who had wanted to please her so badly, he must have worked extra hours to earn the money to pay for it.

Guilt flushed her body as she remembered the hours of resentment she had felt when work had kept him from her side. The lonely meals eaten when he had sent a message home that he had to stay late to finish a brief. And he did all that so he could surprise her with a home of their own as he had promised when he had asked her to marry him. Now she wished she could see him one more time and thank him for being such a considerate husband and provider, so conscientious while she had never told him how much she had appreciated his dedication. She felt so unworthy of this gift and promised herself to remember the man who had made it all possible with gratefulness.

CHAPTER TWO

To spare expense of a hackney, Sarah walked to Mayfair and found the street she needed, but was several blocks away from Number 9. She continued toward her destination noting the riot of colorful flowers from the gardens she could see, the trimmed hedges, wrought-iron fences and gates, the beautiful homes. Would her new home be as large and imposing? No, it couldn't be. Richard could never have afforded one of these palatial residences, not yet anyway, but there were smaller dwellings mixed in among the more-stately homes. She was sure that would be the case with Number 9.

She passed nursemaids taking their charges to the fenced park set aside for those living in the area. Their friendly manner as they met one another at the gate and benches. Finally, even if she had to share it with others, she would have a coveted garden. It would be a place where she could go and sit and read without paying for the right to sit on the bench. She heard sounds of horses, although they must be kept out of sight in the mews, and the breeze that blew down the street held no taint of stable or animal dung. Such a difference from where she lived at the moment. She noticed the street had been swept clean and the droppings disposed of away from where walkers would be assaulted by the smell. The simple differences of living in Mayfield.

Her heart beat faster and, although the numbers on

the houses were in the thirties, they were decreasing quickly. The closer to central Westminster she got the lower the numbers. Number twenty and she began looking ahead, trying to see what was there, who her neighbors would be. She tried to moderate her pace, to be inconspicuous as she fisted her gloved fingers around the key in her hand.

She slowed her steps. There it was—Number 9. White with Corinthian pillars holding up a Greek styled portico entrance over a wide door and the number nine in brass over it. She didn't want to intrude in case the old owners were still in possession so she used the knocker and tipped her head trying to hear a servant inside hurrying to the door.

No sound answered, and she tried again before slipping the key she held tightly in her hand to find the lock opened silently. She peered in seeing furniture in the entrance area and called out in warning if there was someone else there. Leaving the door ajar in case she needed to make a hasty retreat upon finding there were still people living there, she entered a generous sized foyer.

After seeing the quality of the furniture, she hoped the house had been sold partially furnished. If so, it would have been a boon and just one more thing she would be thankful for to dear Richard.

She walked into the parlor, some furniture still under Holland covers, while a cozy sitting area in front of the fireplace met her gaze. Also, an unusual fur lay in front covering much of the floorspace. An odd sort of decor for a formal parlor although that didn't mean she had to leave it there. She could bring over what she already owned and add it making the room just that much more comfortable. If she found there was too much furniture, she would sell the extra. All this appeared fairly new and should be able to be sold through a consignment shop near the warehouse district. She would peek under the dust-covers after she checked the upstairs.

Leaving the kitchen and back rooms for later, she moved up the stairs to see how many bedrooms were there. She found two empty rooms along with a box-room which held a couple of cases and a trunk. Sarah felt she should not intrude into those in case they were being held for the past owners and continued to the last door. When opening it, she gasped. What a truly decadent room. Certainly, one made for lovemaking and not much else.

Flocked paper of red and pink design covered the walls with gold gilt cove-molding and plaster trims. Lamps were set on every flat surface, their crystal pendulums hanging from the circular red glass shades. There were mirrors placed strategically around the bed and, to her horror and amusement, one even hung over the bed.

Oh my, she was sure this wasn't something her husband would have selected. It had to be from the previous owners, probably why he hadn't shown her the house yet. This sort of thing would have had to be removed prior to his showing it to her as their new home. Her very proper husband would never have brought her here to see it in this condition.

She could imagine Richard's embarrassment when he first walked through the house prior to buying it. As she took in the sheer garments hanging on the door a niggle of doubt ran up her spine. Who would move out and leave anything so personal? And that scent. A female's perfume without a doubt although it smelled familiar. Perhaps even with the Holland covers she saw in the room off the foyer the people still lived here. She backed out of the room feeling like a voyeur and hurried down the stairs.

Once more near the entrance, she turned in the opposite direction from the parlor and pushed open one of the double doors. The floor was covered by a large paint-spattered canvas. Instead of the dining table and chairs that would have been in the room, there were stacks of canvases, some began then discarded. She saw the penciled outline of a person. No, not simply a person, but a nude male, his buttocks clearly delineated along with his legs as he faced away from the artist. There were others of a woman, her hair long and covering some strategic intimate area, and then she found one of both of them gazing at one another.

This portraiture was the most complete, and she stood gasping as she recognized her husband's face in profile even though his prominent chin cleft was not showing. The rest of him—naked and entwined with a woman who was also nude. Not a full-on view, but Sarah would know that aquiline nose anywhere, the way the brows winged over his eyes, the pouty bottom lip. A handsome man, attractive and rather charismatic.

She needed to make sure and searched through the canvases lining the room's floor. The most damning was a portraiture of her husband. He was smiling at the artist as if he hadn't a care in the world. His arm with its shirt sleeve rolled up past his elbow resting on a raised knee. The neckline unbuttoned and his hair was mussed. He appeared so carefree. His expression was of a man in love—so smitten he couldn't keep the emotion from radiating out of the paint. Had she ever seen him so happy? So untroubled?

Sarah felt an interloper. These two people had had a love she could only covet. Would he have been like that young man in the portrait all the time if she hadn't been Richard's wife? This many canvases must mean they had known one another for quite a while—and in less than a formal manner. Her gaze returned to the portrait and couldn't imagine ever seeing him like that. Certainly not during their two years of marriage nor the two years prior to that while Richard was getting established in the law firm. He always seemed so serious and concerned with the future, rather, his future.

She had felt so special when he had asked for her hand. After all, she had only a small dowry from her father, also a solicitor until his death soon after she married. Her future husband had assured her they would be the perfect couple and her father could be of benefit to Richard's career. Of course, being the son-in-law to a popular attorney was good for Richard's chosen profession, and he quickly rose within his own firm's office. And Sarah would have been more help if Richard had ever agreed to invite his colleagues home for dinner or found events for them to attend together as a couple.

To find out he had been having an affair was more than a shock. The only seating in the room was the linen draped fainting couch used in the paintings. She would collapse on the floor before she would sit where her husband and his lover had rested. She turned away from the proof of his deceit, the proof her marriage had been a sham to possibly cover the affair from the beginning. She hated thinking that way, but by the number of canvases present and the room upstairs... This had been going on much longer than a few months.

How had she not known—or at least suspected? They had only been married two years, so where had she failed him? When had he become so bored or so tired of her that he took a lover and spent what little free time he had with this other woman? Wait. Did he even waste any time being just her husband? Had he been involved with this woman right from the beginning? Those evenings cut short because he had to return to the office or the cancelled engagements with her supposedly due to needing to confer with clients or other counsel? Had it all been a lie from the day of their betrothal?

Her thoughts in a turmoil, she pushed everything out of her mind so she could concentrate on getting out of there. Away from the proof her husband had never loved her, that her marriage had been a charade of some sort, that Richard had used her to cover up this affair. The horrible thoughts struck her as she fumbled with the doorknobs, pulling them open and running into a wide male chest directly in front of her blocking her exit to the foyer.

Could this day get any worse? Now she would be confronted with someone who probably knew her shame. That she couldn't keep her own husband of only two years by her side and in her bed. But no, that wasn't true. Richard had spent at least one night a week in her bed or, at least, he used to. Perhaps lately it had been less, but he had been so busy working…or so he had said.

What a fool! She tried pushing past the firm chest never peeking up, not wanting to have anyone witness her mortification, the fact she had been betrayed.

A deep voice commanded, "Wait a moment, please. I need to speak with you." Large hands came up on each side of her and clasped onto her upper arms preventing her from any progress as he peered over her head into the room of canvases and her humiliation.

She pushed at his hands, but he wouldn't move and easily kept her in place as she felt him turn to take everything in at a glance. Everything that had taken her several minutes to ascertain. She could not look at his face. Did not want to see either pity or condemnation for not being able to satisfy her husband. Her lips trembled, but otherwise she stood waiting for his censure.

Instead, he led her across the black and white checkered marble floor to the mundane parlor although that fur in front of the fireplace brought a whole new image to mind now she knew what this house was. What it must have meant to her husband.

Pushing her onto the sofa, the unfamiliar man peered around before going to a crystal decanter and pouring some of the golden liquid into a glass next to it. "Here, drink this before you faint on me. I have enough to take in at the moment, although I think you have as well."

Her shaking hands finally brought the glass to her lips, but the fumes reached her nostrils first, and she turned her mouth away.

His rough words sank in. "Drink it. I think we'll both feel better once you do."

She took a sip, coughed, then finished it when he told her to do so. He took the empty glass and refilled it, this time with double what he had given her and drank it down in one long swallow. Sarah took the time to take note of her companion. He was tall, taller than Richard by several inches and broader. She remembered hitting his chest as if it had been a brick wall while he stood and took her weight easily. He was in profile, and she saw that his nose was straight, his brows thick, but nicely tapered over clear grey eyes. He glared at the empty glass as if trying to decide whether to refill it before setting it on the table once again.

"There, I think that helped us both. Now may I inquire who you are?"

Seeing his face full on for the first time, she knew her mouth fell open. This was her house so what right did he have in asking her anything and what made him think to expect an answer?

"Who are you, sir?"

His eyes narrowed as if trying to read something into her question and then blew out a breath. After taking in her black widow weeds in a withering glance, he said, "I'm the cuckold husband of the woman I believe your husband was having an affair with."

Her gaze went to the floor unable to keep his piercing glare any longer. "I'm, ah, I'm sorry. I recently found out about…this place." She allowed her gaze to move around the room, but couldn't allow it to land on this man. Not any part of him although she did note his stick pin glittering with some kind of stone, possibly a garnet as her gaze passed over him.

"I wasn't sure, of course, but I had to find out. Remove anything incriminating, but it took me a while to find someone willing to tell me where she went when I was away."

"Away? You left her alone so she could come after my husband instead?" Sarah, staring at the man, realized how handsome he was and then questioned why any woman would think to wander from him. But perhaps if ignored long enough any woman would wander.

He disregarded the accusation. "I think I've been

able to piece things along, and this has been going on for quite a while. Have you been married long?"

"It would be two years this next month." She couldn't help but gaze around the room again and said in almost a whisper, "I thought this was to be a surprise anniversary gift. Our own home where we could start our family."

She heard his frustration as he exhaled noisily. "I'm sorry to be witness to your pain, madam. I recently found out my wife has been seeing your husband for over the past two years. In fact, even before she and I were married more than four years ago."

"Then why didn't they simply marry one another? They were both free to do so. Why bring pain and embarrassment to so many others?"

"That was probably my fault, I'm afraid. I had been seeing Alicia, a Viscount's daughter, and I'm sure she felt I was the better choice at the time. I understand your, um, husband was not financially able to support her in the manner she wished to become accustomed." She hadn't imagined the inspection he had given her clothing. The dress wasn't new, of course, Aggie had dyed it when they found out Richard had been killed in a carriage accident. It was the best the woman could do on short notice, and it had been one of Sarah's better gowns.

"I was willing to wait for him to become a barrister." She nodded remembering his explanation that it took years for his work to pay off, but that his employer wanted a married man. Someone who was settled and ready to put in the extra time needed to become a barrister. "I knew we would sacrifice some of the extras, but he assured me there would be more once he reached his desired station in his profession. I thought it a perfect life…"

"Alicia wasn't as patient, I'm afraid. She informed me she was with child, and I asked for her hand immediately."

Without thinking about what that made of this man's early relationship with Richard's lover, she exclaimed, "Oh, you have a child? How could a mother be so careless? I hope you both can get past this if only for the child's sake."

He glanced toward the window and cleared his throat. "That won't be possible…"

"No, really, I think if you forgave her, any mother would want to make her marriage work. She will come back to you now that my, um, now that Richard is no longer here."

"It won't be possible, madam, because Alicia died alongside your husband. I was able to hush-up the fact they were together when his carriage missed the turn— but they had been together. They had spent the afternoon at a country inn. On their way home, a dog chased a rabbit under the horses' hooves making them bolt and your husband, who was driving, lost control."

The statement was given without much emotion other than possibly anger. Of course, a man would be when speaking of his wife's lover, a man who seemed to have been a part of the man's marriage since its conception. What had the two people involved been thinking? Were they planning on continuing for years? Buying this house should have proven Richard's commitment to the relationship. After all, his mistress had a house while she, his own wife, remained in a rental. Peering around she knew she would never move into this one. In fact, she wanted to leave now she knew more about her husband than she ever had before. To be truthful—too much.

The man's voice interrupted her thoughts. "I am sorry for your loss. Hell, I'm sorry for my loss although she wasn't much of a wife or a mother. I'm not sure the last time Mary saw Alicia for more than a brief encounter. Probably when the nursemaid brought the child down before dinner."

If she thought the shock of finding her husband's love-nest couldn't be more wretched, she had been wrong. How horrible it would have been to have everyone know. How would she have faced all those mourners and pretend a loss she hadn't felt. In fact, her entire body was beginning to be numb as she learned more about a man she thought she knew everything about. A man she had tied her life to and who she had accepted his ideas and thoughts as her own. Accepted that he knew what was best for her...for their life together.

"Madam? Hell, and damnation, I cannot keep calling you that. Please, allow me a first name so I will not have to voice that man's name again."

She nodded, feeling a fog come over her mind and a blurriness surround her. "Of course, I understand, my name is, Sarah. I would think you knew that as you know so much else about Richard."

"I was focusing on the man. I received some information from the undertaker and the rest from my wife's personal maid and a footman who used to accompany her here several times a week."

"Several times a week? Does that mean she met my, er, Richard, here that often?"

"It would seem so. Sometimes he was here first, and

other times she waited for him. She must have used this place as an artist studio, also. I didn't realize she had this one." He came closer and peered into her eyes as if ascertaining her previous knowledge of the information he was divulging. "My wife wanted to continue to paint, and I thought she was having classes with a professional. I found out she had stopped meeting with the instructor months ago and had been painting here instead. I never questioned her since there was always paint under her fingernails as well as the overwhelming scent of her perfume to cloak the odor of linseed oil on her person."

"That's why her fragrance was so familiar. I think I must have smelled it on my husband some nights when he arrived home late. Foolishly, I thought it was some sort of cigar or pipe tobacco others smoked around him at his club."

"Do not chide yourself too much. It took me months to figure out I was not the father of my daughter although I couldn't love her more."

"Not the fa…?" She felt herself go cold and grabbed onto the sofa's arm to keep from pitching forward. "You think Richard was. You think he allowed your wife to palm off his natural child?"

"Mary is a lovely little girl with a quiet manner and has a cleft in her chin. Usually, one parent must have a cleft for a child to have one. Neither Alicia nor myself has one."

Nodding, Sarah confirmed his suspicion. "Richard had a very prominent cleft."

"I noted as much when I saw the portrait in the other room." His eyes went to the open doorway onto the foyer. "Are you all right, Sarah? It seems to me you are listing."

She put out her hand and righted herself. "I'll be fine. I might have missed a meal or two in the last couple of days. I have been very busy."

"Let me see if there is any food or at least tea here. Don't try to get up just yet."

In the quiet she wondered why she was still there, sitting in her husband's house speaking with a strange man about the most personal of subjects. Before she could find the strength to stand and make her way out, he returned.

"I said to remain seated." He pushed her back against the settee, and she went like a rag doll without a will of her own. "I didn't find much, but there is tea if I get the fire in the stove restarted. It doesn't appear as if anyone else was here. I think Alicia's maid kept things tidy when no one else was around."

"I don't think I could have swallowed anything out of that kitchen anyway. I am sure I am recovered enough to get a hackney and return home." She went to stand again, and this time he allowed her to. It took a moment to figure out how to leave the room, but by that time whatever she thought left of her pride was gone. Besides, this man was the least of anyone who should look down on her or pity her. After all his wife was not only faithless, but he had been unaware of it for the same period of time.

"You will ride back in my carriage, Sarah. I won't allow you to try to make it on your own. Do you have servants at home when I get you there? Someone to take care of you?"

She pulled her arm out of his hand and ungraciously answered him. "I am fine on my own. I am not that destitute I cannot pay my own fare home."

He stopped her with a mere touch. "I did not mean to infer any such thing. But you have had a shock and recently buried your husband. I have had time to realize the truth of the matter while you are still trying to do so. I would not feel right sending you off on your own even if my face is the last one you wish to see at this moment."

She knew she was being discourteous and taking out her anger on the man least needing it. "I am sorry. You are very right in that I am having difficulty taking this all in. Only it is so opposite of what I thought I would find here today. I suppose I can sell it, but somehow it all seems so tawdry, so unclean. I don't think I can accept the funds from its sale."

She handed him the key so he could lock the door and let him escort her to the street where there was an open carriage waiting. His tiger handed him the reins and jumped onto the back step.

"Who are you again, sir? I am afraid I never got your name."

"Hargrove. Lord Hargrove, but I imagine you can call me Henry since we seem to have closer connections than most."

"Lord Hargrove? Then you are an earl. I think I met your wife at an art gallery opening. My husband told me he had a client involved with it, and we went to see the paintings. She was a sponsoring patroness and one of the artists in the event, but I remember them all being of flowers, not portraits. How foolish not to have seen what was right in front of my eyes." So much she had missed. Possibly more if she thought longer on it.

"Don't chastise yourself overly much. I was married to the woman, and she kept me in the dark long enough."

"I am sorry I brought it up. Please forgive my self-absorption. I only seem to see this from my perspective. You have lost a wife and your children, a mother."

"As I said, I have had more time to come to terms, plus I knew there was someone else. As long as she was discreet, I looked the other way. I have my heir and my daughter, so I was content although that does not mean I wanted her name bandied about. After all, my children should remember their mother in the best of light. No one need know about her peccadillos."

"I understand, and you needn't fear I will say anything to anyone." Two motherless children, and one an orphan if she only knew it. Her heart broke thinking of their loss.

"Oh, this is my house just here, thank you." As the carriage stopped, she motioned for the tiger to aid her descent. "Stay in place, my lord. I would rather not have to answer neighbors' questions as to who dropped me off today."

He nodded and drove away as his tiger grabbed onto the rear of the carriage.

CHAPTER THREE

How could he not have known about the house? Had he become so complaisant with his marriage he'd given up worrying about the consequences of his wife's infidelity? Although he was sure it was only with this same man, to say they were discreet was an understatement. They both had something to lose if it had become common knowledge. What little he had been able to find out about this other man confirmed Alicia had been consumed by a need to be with him, even providing Henry with a son so she could be free to dally.

Perhaps it was his fault. Perhaps if he had questioned her more when she had told him about her first pregnancy, she would have confessed the truth and married the man she could evidently be faithful to, Richard Harris, Esquire. A man who was so in love with Alicia he had married another woman to keep others from realizing what was truly going on.

Possibly they had been too careless in the beginning and others had noticed or his employer wanted Harris to have a wife who could act as a hostess as Harris climbed the steps to barrister. The man worked for a very prestigious law firm, and Harris seemed keen to acquire the position soon after leaving university. Everything Henry had learned about the man spoke of someone bent on being best in his field. Having a long-term affair with a nobleman's wife would not endear him to many, most especially his employer, Sir William, who Henry knew as a stickler for convention.

But Henry hadn't lied when he told Mrs. Harris his wife did not have patience and wanted what she wanted quickly. He had put few restrictions on Alicia once she had given him a son as had been the agreement. Alicia would remain faithful until a son was born, and after Henry would allow her to be discrete. His wife was never out of sight of someone loyal to Henry. His son must never face any conflict when ascending to the earldom.

The agreement included anything his wife could desire. She had the freedom of his wealth, as well. She could get anything through his man of business or placed on his accounts, which were many throughout London. Of course, he expected the high cost of dressing her and the expense of the art supplies, although pricey, was less cost than his stable of horses. The fee of the art master was substantial, but it seemed better than having her running about. Bored wives are the bane of a husband, and he thought her interest in Harris had been over upon their marriage.

Arriving at his townhouse, he pulled the team to a stop and handed the reins over to the tiger before jumping down. As he entered the house, his mind was on the woman he had met this afternoon. She wasn't anything as he thought she would be.

After finding his wife had died in an accident accompanied by a married man, he thought the other woman involved would be dowdy or, at least, plain. That she was someone who hadn't taken care of herself and had driven her husband to abandon his vows and accept what Alicia was offering. As soon as he saw the man involved lying on that cold slab in the mortuary, he remembered seeing him with Alicia before they had married. A man he thought had been left behind once Alicia had married him while carrying his child.

Once the daughter was born, Henry noticed his wife's change of attitude toward him. Shunning him from her bed and complaining she didn't want to bear another child so soon. He understood and stayed in his bachelor room while his wife recovered from the birth. Meanwhile, he fell in love with the little girl he had named Mary and spent much of his time each evening with the child before leaving for his nightly entertainments.

He never ran into Alicia during those visits but thought his wife spent time with Mary earlier in the day. After questioning the nursemaids, he realized his wife had never called to see the baby. When he approached Alicia about the failure as he saw it, she brushed off his concerns.

"She's too young to know me from the nursemaids, and I don't have time to change clothes after she spits up on me. It's disgusting, and I don't want that smell to follow me for the rest of the day." The face she made screwing up her mouth thinking about it had not been attractive.

His thoughts were of the child. "Is she ill often? Perhaps we should call in the doctor."

"How should I know? I just told you she is too young to even know whether I visit with her or not. Once she gets old enough for me to dress up, then I'll pay more attention to her. I mean, won't it be cute for us to wear matching dresses and bonnets while driving through the park? I cannot wait." It was the most enthusiasm he had heard coming from his wife about anything in months.

He had been reassured that she seemed excited to interact with their daughter at a later date.

His memories were interrupted by the nursemaid bringing Mary into the library where he often sat before going in to dinner.

"My lord, I've brought Lady Mary down for her visit."

"Thank you, Lucy." Then, putting his arms out, waited for the hug from the little girl as she ran into them. "Well, Sugarplum, what have you been up to today?"

"We practiced reciting some poems, and then I saw a bunny in the garden. Can we keep him? Please?"

He stared into her eyes. "What did nurse say?"

"She said it would bite me and was a dirty animal with fleas and mice."

"Mice?" He peered over at the woman sitting quietly in a chair waiting for the visit to end.

"Lice, my lord. They carry fleas and lice."

"Hm-m-m, nurse might be right, Sugarplum. Wild animals get pests that pets don't. Perhaps we can search for some kittens in the hayloft. The stable master will know if we have any."

"Oh, they're as soft as bunnies, I think. Thank you, Papa, I'll be real good and wait quietly."

He couldn't help the grin that spread across his face. "I know you'll try to, Sugarplum, and I won't make you wait too long. How about tomorrow morning before I need to leave for the day?"

The little girl jumped up and down before her nurse called her to order and she settled down with a wide smile. "I will be ready to go out right after my porridge."

"That should be time enough to find them and play for a little while. Nurse, you can stay in the house. No need for you to climb through the hay trying to find kittens."

"Yes, my lord. I'll have the little miss ready about eight."

While petting three small furry kittens, Mary's brows drew down in worry.

Henry was always watchful of her moods. "What's the matter, Sugarplum? Aren't the kittens soft enough?"

"Yes, they're very nice, but I was worried that their mother ran off."

"Not far. She's right over there watching that we don't hurt her babies. She'll come back as soon as we leave." He watched knowing something was bothering his daughter and waited for her to build up enough courage to put words to her worries.

"I think Michael misses Mother. Is she done being in heaven yet?"

He didn't want to have a discussion about how long Alicia would be away, but worried over his daughter's question. "Is he crying more than usual? Is that why you think he misses her?"

"No, but he feels sad inside, and I miss seeing her pretty dresses and how good she smells. I was hoping she would take me with her one day to see all the clothes like she promised. She said there were stores where one could buy anything one wanted." She peeked through her lashes. "Do you think you could buy a new mother for us?"

His heart felt like it weighed double what it had a minute ago. How to explain to a child that not having her mother wasn't going to bring much change in her life. In any of their lives, but Mary evidently felt what little she did see of her mother was now a hole in her limited social life.

"Hm-m-m-m, I will check into that, Sugarplum. So, you miss your mother now that she's gone?" He tried to read his daughter's expression knowing she had rarely seen her mother when she was alive. "Is that what you want? A new mother?"

"Well, if I could get one like Cook, or possibly even Nurse. She's not too bossy when it's only me and her."

He hid his smile as he pet a small furry head with the tip of one finger. "And Michael. I suppose he misses seeing the dresses, too?"

"No, silly, he's a boy, and he won't wear them when he's older. He'll wear the same as you and ride horses and go to parly, parly…"

"Parliament. But what about you? Why are you asking about a new mother?"

"Because Nurse said I will be getting a governess soon and she will need to go and work somewhere else in the house. Everyone is leaving me."

"Things do change as we grow. I hadn't realized there had been talk of a governess so soon, but I suppose it is time. Even if you get a governess, it doesn't mean you'll not see Lucy any longer. We could set up a time each week for you to spend time with her—just the two of you." Knowing there would be half days off for any governess, he felt confident in saying Lucy would be the person caring for Mary during that time. Michael's nursemaid would be needed for another year at least.

"So, I won't get a new mother?" she asked rather sadly ignoring the little mews of discontent from the kittens she was now ignoring.

"As I said, I'll check into it—for Michael. We wouldn't want him to be sad."

"Thank you, Papa, I know I'll like this new one." She went back to petting the kittens, and he watched the top of her head wondering exactly what his daughter had meant by that. That her hope for a new mother would mean a difference for her, also.

For some reason the expression on Sarah's face floated across his mind. How sad she had appeared when speaking of the children now without their mother. In fact, she had spent more time grieving for their loss than she had her own. The only time he thought she was about to cry was when they had spoken of his daughter.

The woman had shown some animosity toward her unfaithful husband, but nothing that showed great loss. She had regretted not having children, though, and Henry understood that, considering her husband had fathered a daughter with another woman.

He brushed hay from his daughter's long curls and smiled at how lucky he was to have two children to love and cherish. At least he had Alicia to thank for those blessings.

CHAPTER FOUR

"Sarah, a Lord Hargrove is at the door requesting to meet with you. What should I do?" Aggie asked from the doorway to the entryway.

Sarah raised her hand to her hair to check if it was still tucked into the twist at the back of her head. "See him in, Aggie, and wait to see if we'll need tea. If not, simply leave us. I'll be fine alone with him."

Aggie appeared as if she was about to argue then huffed away.

"Mrs. Harris, Lord Hargrove is here." Her woman of all work stood waiting at the doorway into the entry as if she didn't trust anyone with a title.

Sarah stood in greeting. "Welcome, Lord Hargrove, would you care for some refreshments?"

"No, I'm due at my club, and I merely wished to pay my condolences for your loss."

She saw the expression on his face and dismissed Aggie wondering what he really wanted to see her about.

When Aggie left, he took the presumption of closing the parlor door and facing her before asking, "Have you recovered from the shock of yesterday?"

"You mean have I accepted the fact I have been foolish enough to live with a man who was in all intents and purposes married to another? A man who spent what money I saved for a new home on another woman's comfort? A man who was so selfish he denied me a child while fathering one on another woman?"

His brows rose in surprise. "I knew you were more than the shocked woman I met yesterday. Beautiful and feisty. I tip my hat to your stamina."

"I am not sure you are being honest with your praise, my lord. I admit I was flummoxed when I found the home I thought a loving surprise for our anniversary was, in fact, a house shared with another. A woman who already had a lovely home and children and husband." She sat on the chair farthest from the man towering over everything in the room hoping he would sit now that she had.

"I have come to tell you that all signs of my wife have been removed from that house. If you do not wish to move into it, I can have my man of business help you dispose of the property. Although it was known to be a house once owned by a prominent light skirt, no one knew about who had been occupying it for the last two years."

"Two years? That means Richard probably bought that house about the same time he was telling me we couldn't afford a home in a better area even with the dowry my father had given him. I wasn't privy to the contract, but Richard assured me that with those funds we would someday be able to buy a home in Mayfair."

"It seems that it was about that same time, yes. I will return the jewelry he gave my wife, also, of course, or I can have it sold and the funds sent to you."

Her stomach rolled, and she clutched at it with her fist. "I don't want it, any of it. I would rather end up in the street than accept funds procured from the sale of gifts he gave her."

"And is that where you'll end up? In the street?"

She raised her chin. "Possibly, but if I do, I do. I don't have anyone to turn to. Richard didn't like me going out and making friends without him and never brought anyone home. I thought it was because he was ashamed of this house, this address."

"It was probably more that he was afraid someone would question seeing him with Alicia. I found the neighbors in Curzon Street thought they were a married couple and figured they were travelling when they were both gone from the home."

"Oh, that makes some sense, I suppose. Richard wouldn't want to run into people he worked with while he was escorting your wife around town. I assume they did go out together?"

He seemed hesitant with his answer. "It seems they did in areas and places they wouldn't be recognized. That is why they were in the country when the accident occurred."

"It was all such a waste, though, wasn't it? I mean they spent their lives hiding, lying, and sneaking around. I lost a husband and you lost a wife, your children a mother…"

When she raised her head, he said, "I feel blessed to still have my children. I have a five-year-old daughter and a twenty-eight-month-old son. And before you ask, I am sure the boy is mine just as I'm as sure the girl is your husband's child, although I would fight to the death if anyone said the words out loud."

"So, they started up their relationship again soon after your son was born?"

"I watched her closely prior to his conception not wanting a repeat of having another man's child become heir to my title, but Alicia seemed to be content. I really thought they had broken it off with one another. That is until Alicia said she would be willing to try to get an heir if I would accept that as the end of her commitment to me, to the marriage." He rubbed his fingers through his dark hair making him appear much younger than he had before. "I hoped that meant she was ready to try to make the marriage work, but it evidently wasn't. My son was born, and soon after Alicia ignored him as she had Mary and began to complain she wanted to start up her painting again, but required a master artist to train under."

"And that was about the time Richard and I were married? So, when we were saying our 'I do's' he was already thinking of your wife." She seemed disheartened by how naive she had been. "Now I know where my dowry went. How could I have been so foolish?"

"Don't think of yourself as foolish. I truly believe your husband was going to try to make the marriage work, but as soon as Alicia realized he was getting married she purposely set out to meet with him. I'm sorry my uncaring of what my wife got up to at the time caused your heartache."

"I'm not so sure one could call it heartache." She noticed the drawing down of his brows and continued to explain, "I thought I loved Richard at the time we were betrothed, but it soon became apparent when he was gone so often, I didn't miss him. I missed my father much more and the loss of my dream."

"Your dream? It wasn't to marry and be a good wife as most women dream?"

"In a way, but I wanted to make a home and be a mother. My own died when I was young, and my father was everything to me, but I wanted children to love. It was the only reason I accepted Richard's proposal. He told me children and a home life were important to him, too."

Henry stood and paced in the small space between the chair and the fireplace. "I feel somewhat responsible for this whole fiasco. If I had prevented Alicia from straying, held her back more, she might not have been able to return to your husband. I simply didn't care any longer, accepted I had made a grave error in judgement, and spent my time caring for my son who had been born early and didn't grow very quickly. Not as quickly as Mary had, and the doctor said it was due to Alicia not taking care of herself and eating as she should during the pregnancy."

"Do you think she did it on purpose? I mean was she that unhappy while being with child?"

Again swiping his fingers through his hair, he shook his head. "I cannot be sure, of course. She complained of getting fat which I tried to assure her she wasn't and that she would have marks left on her body from carrying a second child which I assured her I wouldn't notice. I still wasn't aware of her interest in any other man, so didn't understand her worries. It was all about her appearance to the man she really wanted to be with. The only man she evidently wanted to see her body—your husband."

He glanced up and saw her mortification. "I am sorry, Sarah. For some reason, I feel we are in this together, a secret we both must keep or face possible censure. I don't want any of this to come back on the children. They both are innocent of any wrong doing, although society would taint their lives forever if gossipmongers decided to check into the accident. Even Michael's parentage could be under scrutiny if any of this got out."

"If you and I are the only ones to know, it will not get out, I can assure you. Can you trust the lady's maid and footman even though they know your son was born before your wife and my husband took up together the second time? They wouldn't know about your daughter, would they?"

"I trust them both to keep quiet about the affair and the house on Curzon Street. Neither had even met Alicia until after my marriage, so there would be no reason to question my children's parentage. After today, I hope never to have to discuss it ever again."

"Will you never tell your daughter?"

"I can't see there being any benefit to do so. Your husband had no progeny for her to run into, and I know he has no close kin besides yourself. Mary won't need to learn of it, and I do not intend she ever question my love and support. From birth she has been my daughter."

Sarah knew she appeared wistful. How much having Richard's child would have helped mend the pain of finding out about her husband's perfidy. How making plans for a child's future would have given her something to think about besides the feeling of being used and tossed aside as she had been.

"Could I see her? Mary, I mean. Perhaps when her nurse takes her for a walk or something. I won't talk with her, say anything, but I feel I need to see her."

He gazed at her and nodded. "Sarah, I would like you to meet both children. You are the closest relative to Mary, and I would like her to know you in case something ever happened to me. Possibly become her Godmother."

Her heart swelled, and tears pricked her eyes. "Are you sure? How do we explain me?"

"That you knew her mother and father, and I have asked you. Now that I am a widower, people will not question my need to have someone I trust look after my children if I were unable to do so. No one will ask why, and I think you would be a kind Godmother if she ever needed one."

"I would love to meet her, meet them both although Michael might be too young to remember when he gets older. If you still think the same after we meet, then I accept the position as Mary's Godmother and will look after her spiritual needs if anything should happen to you."

He smiled for the first time since entering the room. "I feel much lighter now that we have come to some decision. I believe this is the right path, and I should have thought of it sooner instead of worrying about leaving you behind."

He opened the door before she could formulate any question or denial. Bowing, he turned and let himself out the front door while placing his hat back on his clearly tussled hair.

Sarah paced her entry which consisted of three steps both directions and glanced at the mirror next to the door. Her reflection showed a very unfashionable woman. She wore her black dress, but had refused to decimate her only spring bonnet by tearing off the flowers and ribbons to replace them with black. She hadn't slept last night so appeared tired. It wasn't due to grief, but worry over her reaction to seeing Richard's daughter. A little girl who would be proof of her husband's ongoing deceit.

A message was sent by Henry, rather Lord Hargrove, for Sarah to expect a carriage outside her door this morning. Ever since receiving that note she had been on pins and needles unsure of how to act when meeting the little girl. The baby she was much less worried about even if she didn't know much about babies. She knew at that age there wouldn't be much she could say or do he would remember.

A light knock on the door heralded her ride, and she sucked in a deep breath before opening the door and meeting a footman wearing the same livery as the tiger of the prior day. Before the man could say anything, she grabbed her reticule and parasol saying, "I am ready now. No need to keep the horses waiting."

He seemed surprised and hastened to get in front of her to hand her into the open carriage before raising the step and climbing-up in back with the driver. Sarah leaned back onto the soft squabs and admired the workmanship of the stitching and buttoning of the seat facing her. This certainly wouldn't be mistaken for a hackney cab having an odorous interior and cloudy window glass.

The breeze coming down the street cooled her heated face. She hoped it wasn't as red as it felt from the emotions flowing through her. Worry of how she would feel, what she could say to a child who had recently lost her mother and face a man whose life had been turned upside down through her husband's actions. The direction of the carriage took her to Mayfair, of course, and passing the large homes with hidden gardens forced her to face the realization she would never live in Mayfair, never have the house with access to a central garden, never be a mother.

A few people strolled the streets, nursemaids pushing perambulators and footmen walking small dogs. Tradesmen wearing more modest clothing and carrying boxes of produce or fish were heading to or from the servants' entrances. Liveried footmen striding to do their master's bidding.

The carriage slowed to pull into a curved drive and stopped under a canopy in front of a wide black enameled door with polished brass hardware. It opened immediately as she was handed down by the footman, and a tall, thin butler watched as she approached.

"My lord and his children await you in the back garden, Mrs. Harris. Would you care to leave the parasol with me, or may I carry it for you?"

She had not paused in her stride wondering why the man thought she needed help with a simple parasol. After all, she had been carrying one for herself since she was twelve. "I'll take it with me if you don't mind in case there is too much sun for the children in the garden."

"As you wish, madam."

Sarah hid a smile thinking of what will be said about her at the servants' supper table that evening. She knew she wasn't acting as a titled lady would, but she was who she was and wouldn't alter herself to meet the expectations of others. She was no longer going to do what others thought she should, but what her own thoughts dictated. Holding the unopened parasol like a baton, she gripped it as a lifeline as she passed through the intimidating rooms.

The butler led her through the main halls and into a parlor which had several sets of French style doors leading into the sunny, flowered garden. Giggles welcomed her as she crossed the stone pavers to the open grass area. There she was met by a scene so poignant in its proof of a father's love for his children her throat tightened with unshed tears.

She waved the butler away not wanting her arrival to interfere with the fun being played out by the three family members. Henry was on the grass, stains on his buff-colored breeches showing it wasn't his first time that day. He growled menacingly at a little girl trying to hide behind a flowering bush while covering her mouth to keep the giggles from giving her hiding place away. A toddler, wearing a dress with lace collar plopped down on his bottom and crowed loudly at his father, no sense of fear showing as he pulled up tufts of grass and let them fall to the ground.

Sarah hadn't been noticed yet by any of the three. They were so entranced with one another. As Henry reared up like a horse on his hind legs and pawed the air, Mary squealed and jumped out from her position. "Papa, a dragon doesn't do that. You must stay on your hands and knees while growling. And show your teeth. You're supposed to be scary not laughing."

He fell out of character saying, "How do you know? None of the stories we've read says I can't stand up. Besides think how it would appear to Mrs. Harris to find me wallowing on the grass with you?"

Mary's eyes moved past him, and he turned to where his daughter stared. "She's here already I think, Papa, and she doesn't seem to mind."

He faced Sarah with an expression of chagrin. "You made good time. I expected you a little later after I tired the children out so they would sit quietly with us."

Sarah smiled and sat on a stone bench at the edge of the terrace. "I don't think they must sit quietly. Children need more leniency as to their behavior. Playing with their father is certainly permissible."

He walked toward her brushing ineffectively at the

green smears on his knees. "Jason, my valet, will be beside himself when he sees these breeches." He turned to pick up the baby while waving for his daughter to approach, also. Sarah stood for the introduction.

"Mary, this is the lady I told you about. She is a family friend and wanted to meet you and Michael. Make your curtsy, please."

The girl made a wobbly curtsy in the grass. "How do you do, my lady?"

"Oh, I'm not my lady..."

"I'll explain to her later, Sarah. She has had very little contact with anyone except the nursemaids and servants." He led the children into the shade of the house where there was another bench and sat down with Michael still in his arms. Sarah followed with her eyes eating up the features of the little girl as she followed Henry and the baby.

Searching and finding the many similarities between this child and her dead husband, she was speechless with regret. At first Sarah had feared she wouldn't be able to look at the child without feeling betrayed, but that wasn't how she felt at all. She gazed at this beautiful child and saw the face of her own child if she had ever conceived. The golden hair, the blue eyes with winged brows...the pouty bottom lip was even there keeping guard over the cleft in her little chin.

Those familiar blue eyes watched her taking in every nuance of her face, as well. "Are you going to be my new mother? I was told by Nurse I must be very good so you will like me."

Sarah's breathing became constrained, and she would later have a word with Nurse about scaring this little girl into thinking she would lose a parent merely by being naughty. Didn't the woman think how Mary would take that warning? That she may feel guilt over her mother dying, leaving her due to something Mary had done in the past?

"I'm not going to be your new mother, but your father has asked me to be your Godmother."

A scowl crossed the girl's face. "What is the difference between a mother and a Godmother? They sound the same to me."

"Well, a Godmother is responsible for your spiritual needs and makes sure you are well cared for and loved. I think I will be able to give you much love."

"How is that different from what a mother does?" Mary looked between the two adults.

"Mary, why don't you go with Lucy and get cleaned up before we have our tea. I need to speak with Mrs. Harris while you are gone." Two nursemaids appeared from inside with one taking Mary's hand and the other accepting a wiggling Michael.

Henry, she simply could not think of him as Lord Hargrove no matter how many times she had reminded herself who he is, swiped his fingers through his hair tumbling the neat style. She knew that action meant he was being torn between decisions, unsure which direction to take. She still thought it made him appear much younger than his usual appearance.

He motioned for her to sit as he stood. "I have been thinking about our talk yesterday and am not happy I allowed myself to leave before I approached you on this matter."

"I'm not sure I understand. I thought you wanted me to meet the children, be Mary's Godmother."

"I did, I do. But I want more for you, for us. I think

we should create the family these children deserve. I can see you are taken with Mary and as you heard she is very interested in getting a mother. She has even asked if I were lonely at night after she and Michael are in bed. I was afraid of what she would ask me next." He smiled and then sat next to her. "I never had a mother since I was very young. I thought I hadn't missed having one, but lately I think maybe I have. My father never married again nor brought females home for inspection although I have strong female family members whom I could depend on. No one to take care of these two, though, at their age. I worry about the children's future. Who will take care of them if something happens to me?"

Sarah felt only honesty would be accepted and that this man knew more about her finances than she did. "I can't say I've thought about the future other than to worry over it. I mean, I won't have much money even if I can push myself to use the money from the sale of the house and furnishings. And I hate to let my two home-help go, but I won't be able to keep them for long and make my funds last."

"I can find a place for them both. If not here then at one of my estates if either wants a country life. My concern is knowing whether you can see yourself as a mother to two children who have not really had a mother in their past. I can see you are a caring person. You never ranted and raved about what other women would have considered an unfairness, and you want to be a mother. You seem compassionate toward Mary, and she is in dire need of a woman's care."

"I thought when I saw Richard in that wooden coffin, I was destined to be childless, a widow without funds or future. Now you are asking me to rethink my choices. I must admit I am unsure what it is you are asking of me."

"To be clear, I am asking for your hand in marriage. I want you to be a mother to my two children, a wife to me…"

She wasn't sure what her expression showed, but he quickly added, "That can wait until we know one another better, after your time of grieving is over, when you find you want to be a wife again. My priority is to my children, one I thought would be of interest to you."

She gave him a frown. "They both are of interest to me, sir. Mary has a special place in my heart already, but that doesn't mean Michael is not in need of a mother's love as well."

His brow cleared, and a smile appeared. "It sounds as if you have made up your mind already. May I announce you have accepted my proposal and will become my countess?"

Her stomach plummeted. "Oh, I wish you hadn't said that, my lord. I cannot think of myself as a countess, and just the word makes me flush with fear."

"You have nothing to worry about. I've seen you under stress and duress, and you were never in fear and always gracious. It's only one of the things I admire about you. You are a mother my children will be proud of as they grow and learn to appreciate all you will bring to our lives."

She blushed hearing him add his admiration. Did he really think she was a good candidate for his countess? He barely knew her and knew nothing about her dreams, how she had wanted a large family and a large country home to raise them in.

He watched her and added, "I hope, with time, you

will want to add to our family. I always saw myself with a large family. I have several estates that go begging for the sound of children's laughter. I find it is more than time they were filled with young people, ponies, and all sorts of games and sports."

For a moment, she wondered if she had spoken her thoughts aloud then honed in on her one major fear. "I'm not sure I can live through a husband's infidelity again." Her head shook slowly back and forth. "I know I could not support a husband who could not hold the marriage in as high a regard as my own. I must, for that reason, decline the offer."

"If that is the only reason holding you back from accepting, then allow me to make myself completely understood. When I marry it is forever and to one woman who will hold my attention and my name. I lived with one wife who denied me her bed and wandered with another man, and I never felt I should retaliate in any manner. Certainly not embroiling myself with yet another woman. I didn't in the past and I won't in the future, although I do not think I need worry you will bring me a cuckoo. Does that make my position clear?"

"Yes, yes it does, my lord." Her mind raced through all types of scenarios, possibilities, and dreams. Finally, she heard the children returning and knew she must make a decision. "I will accept your proposal, my lord, and will be the best mother to these children I can be. As far as being your wife, I request your patience and tolerance for my hesitancy to enter into a more intimate relationship so soon. I hope to overcome my inhibitions since I, too, wish for children of my own body if I can be so blessed. I pray you understand my reticence and that it isn't due to any ill feelings toward you or men in general."

"I think that would be the best way to go on. We'll be married by special license, and no one will think much about it since I have young children who need a mother. No one will put together your husband and my wife, and the talk of our quick marriage will die down as we will live a quiet life, possibly in the country, in respect for the ones we have lost."

Mary came running out ignoring her nurse's call for her to act like a lady and plunked down next to Sarah on the bench. Michael put his chubby arms out as soon as he saw his father saying, "Mine, Mine."

Henry reached out and accepted his son, sitting him on his arm like a chair. "Well, there are two shiny faced children." Turning to the nurses he dismissed them until they were called. He saw the butler motion that tea was served in the parlor and he stood, holding out his spare hand to help Sarah. Mary took her other hand and walked beside her.

Inside, Sarah missed the breeze on her face, but enjoyed the opportunity to interact with Mary and Michael. She was surprised when Henry handed off the baby to her while he poured tea for them all and set a plate out for each child giving Mary a cup of tea which was mostly warm milk and sugar.

Sarah smiled at Henry conspiratorially as Mary behaved like the treat was one most sought after. Henry sat next to Sarah and helped her balance her cup as well as a baby eager to grab anything that caught his attention which changed moment by moment. After keeping the cup of tea from toppling once again, Henry drained his cup and took the baby onto his lap.

She chuckled. "I don't know how mothers get any nourishment with young ones at hand." She too drank her now cold tea quickly so the danger of a spill would be out of the reach of the hand-waving toddler.

"I found having tea with these two meant I should drink a cup downstairs quickly before joining them. I wear more jelly tarts than eat them, I'm afraid, and have to face Jason's complaints and laments over my wardrobe."

"I can't imagine anyone taking you to task over jelly smears and grass stains." Smiling, she handed Michael a piece of buttered muffin and watched as he smashed it into his open mouth blowing a shower of crumbs as he laughed in glee with his prize.

Henry held a cup of milk to his son's little mouth and, after trying to blow bubbles, Michael was coaxed into taking a drink. Finally, the adults thought the children were as fed as they were going to get and took them back to the garden.

Michael was by now showing his need for a rest and laid his head on his father's shoulder.

"I think I need to speak with Mary privately before we continue with any plans, my lord."

He nodded and moved to the end of the bench, but within hearing. Sarah approved his need to know exactly what was being said.

"Mary, will you sit next to me for a while, please?" The young girl happily climbed on the bench then faced forward with her little legs hanging over the edge.

With a quick glance toward Henry, Sarah began her explanation. "Mary, your father has asked me to become his wife which would mean I would also be your mother."

"Truly? I knew Papa was bringing you here for a reason. He is the best of papas and makes me happy all the time. I'm sure you're going to like it—being my mother. I'll be very good from now on." The little girl's blue eyes were beseeching in their plea for Sarah to believe her.

"Mary, although I like you very much, I know it is difficult to be good all the time. I will not leave you because you may do something less than perfect or act naughty. And I never want you to think that is why your mother isn't here right now. I am sure she would rather be here with you than anywhere else."

"Papa said she is in heaven. That she was caught in an accident and died." Mary watched closely to how this information was accepted by the woman next to her. Biting her bottom lip in worry.

Sarah nodded. "I am very sorry that happened, but I would be very happy if you thought we could rub alongside one another. You see, I don't have any children, and you don't have a mother. Do you see how maybe your father would think we would be good for one another?"

The little blonde head nodded. "Do you want to meet my doll, Anne Marie? Papa brought her back from Pa-parist, France."

Sarah swallowed, nodding, emotion tightening her vocal cords until she feared she would only croak at the little girl and possibly frighten her. She turned toward Henry and asked without words.

He answered. "Certainly, Mary. Go up and get Anne Marie out of her bed, and we'll both be up to see you."

"All right, Papa, I can do that. I learned the way all by myself, although I think Lucy will be at the top of the stairs watching for me."

"Go along, Poppet, while I speak with your father a

moment." Sarah had finally found her voice and tried not to let the misting of her eyes run in tears down her cheeks while the child was still in the garden.

A clean handkerchief appeared in front of her which she accepted while he asked, "Is this going to be something you can do? Is it too painful to see her, see your husband's features in my daughter?"

"No, it's not that. I saw what my child would have looked like if I had had one." Then she became concerned realizing how strongly the child's traits took after Richard. "Have you never condemned her for being another man's child?"

"Never! Not for a moment, although I had my doubts from the beginning. Mary was a very robust baby when she was born and, although I was expecting an early birth, Mary was exceedingly early considering when Alicia and I first, um, first met."

She bit her bottom lip. "I understand, I think. But you don't seem to differentiate between Mary and Michael."

"No, both children will never hear from me that there is a possibility that their mother was less than she should be or that they were not loved and wanted by me as their father. Right now, I am those children's lone parent, and I cherish them for the gifts from God they are."

"As will I. I promise you now, I will care for and love these children as my own." She could not meet his gaze as she continued, "And if I can, I mean if we are blessed with children, then there will be no difference between any of them in my heart or mind."

He smiled and reached out for her while balancing a now sleeping Michael. "Come, we will put the children down for a rest and then talk about the wedding. I expect this will catch up with you tonight while you're lying in your bed, and I don't want you worrying over little items not covered today."

Sarah was amazed he seemed to know her so well, how her mind worked and how she worried once the lights went out and she was alone with only her thoughts. "I will ask questions until I'm sure I know everything that is to happen."

"Nothing will happen that you don't wish to happen. Remember that and the reason we are getting married. These children need a mother, and I need a woman to stand as my countess, one whom I can trust not to embarrass me or the children by taking a lover."

That was the thought that rose in her mind over the next hour before leaving alone in a carriage just as she had arrived. The children needed her, and she needed them. The wounds inflicted by her late husband when she discovered his perfidy were even now easing. Something she thought would fester for years was already in the past as if washed away by a spring rain shower.

In bed that night, she was amazed at how easily her life was going to change, how she could let her future husband lift the fear and worry of what was to become of her from her shoulders. After years of frugality, Henry told her to buy whatever she needed in way of clothes, to let Aggie and Vernon know they were welcome staff at any of his residences, and anything she thought she needed to bring from her home now would be moved by his own servants. Everything would be covered and taken care of.

It was so easy, possibly too easy. Was she in shock and allowing the numbness she first felt at learning of

Richard's death mask the questions she should be asking? Like—why me? There must be dozens of women, widows and debutants who would make a much better wife for Henry, someone raised with the expectations of becoming a countess from birth. Someone experienced with society and possibly even having a proven track record of producing children. An aristocrat's widow still young enough to give Henry the children he wanted.

After all, she had been married for two years and had never produced a child, never conceived at all. Didn't that mean she wasn't the best candidate as a wife? Should she have brought that fact up this afternoon? Wanting a child and being able to produce one were two very different things.

She let out a half-laugh half-sigh as she realized the irony of her wanting a child and not producing one and Alicia's producing children, but not wanting them.

Remembering what Henry had assured her quieted some of her misgivings. He told her Alicia, although a viscount's daughter, never took any interest in running his home and refused to visit even his closest country estate. Sarah already knew the children had been left to the nurses so if that lady, born to have a title, could manage then there was no reason Sarah could not do so as well.

Although she knew that she would not be content with things as they were, she thought she could learn what she needed. Both Bates, the butler, and Mrs. Cushions, the housekeeper, seemed welcoming when Henry introduced her to them before she left. Sarah was sure they would be lenient with any mistakes she might make along the way. And Aggie had worked in a prominent London ton home and could help Sarah wade through the hierarchy she would face as a countess. Even if they lived quietly, there would be times Henry would need to make appearances within society, and Mary would have her come-out.

Could Sarah make enough excuses not to go to such events without causing undue talk? Bring attention to her marriage and possibly her lack of standing? Being a granddaughter of a Viscount, daughter of a second son of a second son did not give her much status. Her widowed father never mentioned his relationship or the title now held by a far distant cousin. Certainly no one who would acknowledge her.

She punched her pillow into a ball and hoped that would help her gain sleep. She needed to rest at least a few hours before having to rise and tell Aggie about the new plans. Sarah hoped the woman would agree to accompany her to the Hargrove townhouse as her ladies' maid. Sarah needed a sympathetic friend with whom she could confide. Everything except who had fathered Mary and the goings on at number nine Curzon Street.

CHAPTER FIVE

Henry wasn't sure how Sarah would respond to his sending personal items to her home, but he knew she was aware her clothes would not match what would be expected of his wife, his countess. He wanted her to have something pretty, something new. A hat the modiste assured him would be proper for a woman in mourning, black with lavender flowers and matching gloves. He hadn't sent lingerie as such, but he thought silk stockings and ribbon garters might make her feel special on their wedding day. Not that he expected to see either since she had reiterated her need for time to get to know one another better before she could contemplate anything more between them.

He had agreed readily since it was most important to have her marry him, then keep her close until she felt comfortable enough to be his wife in all ways. Not wanting to study his reasons too closely, he continued as if this were a normal engagement.

The common license wasn't difficult for him to obtain, and one of the ministers at St. George was willing to perform the ceremony. He asked his good friend, Lord Markham, to stand as his best man and made sure there would be flowers for both Sarah and whomever she invited to be her witness.

It seemed as if they never had a moment to speak privately since his making the proposal. When Sarah visited, which she had done daily, she spent her time with the children either in the nursery or the garden if it was nice enough. He tried to be at home during those times and even joined in on the games or play with the children. Sarah had a natural way with them, and Mary increasingly spoke about the day when Sarah would become her mother and not have to leave at the end of the afternoon.

He spent this time watching Sarah and searching for any signs she had changed her mind or had second thoughts. Again, he did not study why he was worried. After all, it wasn't as if his heart was invested or that even the children would be heartbroken if, for some reason, she called it off. His children enjoyed having her pay attention to them, but he didn't think their hearts were entangled with hers—not yet, at least.

But was his? He was unable to understand his deep feelings for this woman. She was attractive, but he had met equally attractive women elsewhere. She had a pleasant way of speaking, and he enjoyed listening to her read stories to his children and how she explained nature to them when they spent time in the garden. He liked watching her cross the room to pick out a toy for Michael and had caught himself more than once leaning closer to catch her scent—something between sugar biscuits and jelly tarts.

And he envisioned himself making love to her multiple times and enjoying the experience over and over. He thought that part of his life had ended when Alicia had lost interest in him. Although his body had indicated otherwise from the first contact between Sarah and him as they both searched for answers in that small house on Curzon Street.

See there? That was the kind of thoughts that made him worry he was thinking of her as a woman and not as someone he felt sorry for or who he had an obligation to help since his indifference to his wife's antics had allowed Sarah's husband to be unfaithful. Everything he found out about the man assured Henry that Richard had gone into his marriage for the right reasons if not with undying love.

As Henry cleaned out his wife's personal correspondence, he found letters from Sarah's husband and he hadn't responded as a love-sick swain. In fact, he seemed somewhat angry in the oldest ones, the ones written in answer to Alicia's initial notes. Henry could tell by the progression of the letters that it had taken a while before the man's interest was brought to life again.

At least Sarah didn't need to believe herself to be a dupe since it seems her husband meant to be loyal. Only Alicia was more tenacious and had a stronger pull on the man's heart. The more recent notes were full of sentimental drivel and remorse for ever marrying anyone else. Those letters he wasn't sure he would share with Sarah, but he was torn as to whether to tell her about her husband's reticence in starting an affair with Alicia after Michael's birth.

Henry had found himself torn between burning them or allowing Sarah to read them. Making a final decision, he got rid of any evidence, any hint his wife had been with another man. He never wanted Mary, or Michael for that matter, to learn such things about their mother. Hopefully, everyone who knew anything about the affair would remain closed mouth.

The sound of a carriage stopping outside the front door brought him back to the present and his fiancée's reaction to his gifts. He shot his cuffs and inhaled deeply as he walked to the foyer to greet her and walk her upstairs to the children's rooms.

Sarah accepted Henry's arm and remained silent until they were on the first floor, but had not yet ascended to the nursery on the floor above.

"Lord Hargrove, I wish to acknowledge the packages I received this morning from a very exclusive mantua maker. Although as a married man you may have been accustomed to ordering certain women's garments, I do not feel it proper to accept them. I probably won't feel comfortable doing so even after we are wed."

"I understand and I agree, I over-stepped my bounds. I should have waited until after we were married, although I can assure you the modiste thought nothing of the purchases or that they were sent to a different address than my own."

"And that points out the truly wide expanse in our thinking. I agree a husband may buy certain, special items, but only after the wedding and certainly after they have begun their marriage. We have agreed that we shall not begin, um-m, more intimate behaviors until we both are comfortable with one another."

He tried to hide a smile which infuriated her to the bone since she was trying to set the ground rules and he was already reneging on the first and most important one she had made. She stamped her foot which barely made a sound on the thick carpet making her even angrier.

"Lord Hargrove, you must take me seriously!"

He turned her to continue toward the next floor. "I do take you seriously, and I understand that I may have purchased items that only a husband should buy for his wife. I saw them, and I thought you would enjoy having something new for our special day."

She felt herself soften toward him. "Everything was lovely, and I want to look nice for you, to appear a countess in case anyone you know happens by. I guess I'm irritated that for years I denied myself anything not practical or able to withstand dozens of washings because I thought we couldn't afford them. I even had a savings account of coins accumulated in a jar at the back of the kitchen cupboard. It isn't much although I was so excited thinking about the time, I would show it to Richard and we would celebrate and choose something to buy for our first home."

"I don't like to see you torture yourself in this manner, Sarah. It makes me sorry I didn't notice all the signs Alicia was having an affair. My disregard of my wife's activities caused you great pain which I wish I could alleviate now."

"You are no more at fault than I am. Our spouses made their choices, and we are the ones left to make something of our lives, for ourselves and for Mary and Michael. I will try not to dwell on what-might-have-been, and I encourage you to do the same. We are looking forward to a new life, one filled with common ground and promise of better things in the future. We are both young enough to begin again, and I am eager to start my life with your children."

"Our children, Sarah." He stopped once at the top of the stairs and held her hand. "And ours when you're ready. As you reminded me, we are still young enough to begin again, only this time for the right reasons. A mutual desire to raise these children in a safe and loving home and to give them siblings when you are ready."

"I worry you will lose patience with me, my lord…"

"Henry. Call me, Henry. I find I like the sound of my name on your lips, and I hope you will find it easier to address me in that manner. I want us to be something closer than merely a married couple. I feel we are already closer than most who may have known one another for years. Our acquaintance came about in an unusual manner, but it has cut through the need for pretense."

"I admit you saw me at my lowest, my most vulnerable. I had no idea Richard was anything besides a dedicated barrister and normal husband. That he kept such secrets from me and I am sure his employer, makes me question everything else about my life." Her future husband still held her hand and squeezed her fingers in acknowledgment.

"I hope all that is in the past where it belongs. I do not ever plan on bringing it up again, and I want you to remember only the good times. We have Mary and we have Michael and whatever other children we are blessed with to continue our family. The fact we have known one another at our lowest point means there is only one way to go." His smile crinkled his eyes, and she looked at him as a man for the first time realizing she would have been attracted to him if he hadn't been the husband of the woman who had had an affair with Richard.

"The children will be getting anxious if we do not put in an appearance soon, my…I mean, Henry. I am to finish the story of the dragon and the prince this afternoon."

He dropped her hand, allowing her to turn toward the closed door. "I remember that very well since I, too, am looking forward to hearing the ending."

CHAPTER SIX

Henry stood in front of the altar beside the minister and resisted pulling on the cravat as it felt tighter and tighter around his neck. It was a warmer than usual day, or at least he thought so, and found himself glancing periodically down the empty aisle toward the large closed doors. His friend stood stoically next to him with the same expression as Henry would have thought a man going to the gallows would have. He didn't know why Markham appeared that way since it was Henry who was tying himself to a woman he hardly knew and who could make his life as miserable as Alicia had.

Markham glanced toward the Piccadilly Street doors and shrugged. "Maybe this is your warning or your opportunity to rethink your decision. After all, she's more than half an hour late."

"She'll be here. I sent my own carriage for her, and someone would have been here by now if she had cried off."

Another shrug. "It's your wedding...or funeral. I'm only here because you promised me Champagne at the wedding breakfast."

Henry knew it was more than that which brought Mark to this dark, humid church on an early Wednesday morning, but it was the only time St. George's had been available. This was one of the most popular venues for weddings of the ton and was usually booked fully months in advance.

He knew his friend was rarely awake at this hour unless he was arriving home from an evening of frivolity. A true friend was hard to find, and Mark had proven his friendship more than once—even had warned him off marrying Alicia.

The warning went unheeded because Mark had admitted he knew nothing substantial and his opinion was based on an inner premonition. His friend hadn't met Sarah yet, but knew some of the background on how Henry had met his future bride. Henry had to tell him something since Mark would question the marriage, the need to marry so soon after Henry had received his freedom. Mark knew every unattached woman Henry had, and suddenly becoming engaged to Sarah raised his friend's interest. Henry felt he needed to explain why the rush into the marital state again after the disaster of his first marriage and found explaining the need of the children to have a loving mother softened even Mark's cold, hard heart.

The doors creaked open, and a ray of sunlight shown across the aisle. The lavender clad figure slipped in along with a much larger robust figure whom he recognized as Sarah's servant, the one she was bringing to his home as a ladies' maid. They made their way toward him as the organ burst into sound.

Everyone besides the minister startled, but then Henry settled back to watch his bride and her witness get in position. They both held the flowers he had sent ahead with his footman, and he smiled encouragingly as she finally made it to his side. He faced the minister and nodded, content Sarah was ready to proceed as well.

The organ stopped as abruptly has it had begun, and

the ceremony proceeded without any further delays. Henry was surprised his bride had accepted half-mourning, but he could not fault the dress. It was splendid and would have made the most critical ton lady unable to voice a disparaging remark. He held her hand part way through the words being spoken and kept ahold of it, rubbing his thumb over the wrist as he calmed her. Or perhaps it was to calm himself.

The wait had seemed excruciating, and his relief when the door had opened and he saw her standing there lightened the feeling in his chest. Once he knew she was safe and still wished to marry him, he allowed the joy he had been holding back full reign. He never let his eyes move off her form as he watched her say her vows, watched her lips form a smile afterwards, watched her eyes as she accepted his ring upon her finger.

He never remembered being so involved with another person in his life, not even his children. The bond he was forging with this woman took his breath away, and he almost missed the minister indicating he could kiss his bride if he so wished. And he wished—very, very much.

He held his emotions in check as he kissed her lips for the first time. A mild salute to the force of emotion simmering beneath the surface. His bride seemed content with it, turning to accept the bouquet of flowers from her lady's maid before turning back to him to take his arm. He led her to the small alcove to sign the register and finish the necessary paperwork before escorting her from the church.

Even though it was barely daylight, there were people outside the church awaiting the coins newly married couples often tossed out to those present. Henry was ready for them and handed a small cloth bag to his footman to disperse while the onlookers sent well wishes and blessings to the united couple.

Handing Sarah onto the seat of the enclosed carriage, he followed and left the rear facing seat for Markham. This was the first time his best friend and his wife will truly meet.

"Lady Hargrove, allow me to be one of the first to personally extend my felicitations. This man you married and I have been very close since our early school years. I hope we can become better acquainted now that I know about your presence in his life."

Sarah seemed taken back at Mark's first words. It must seem strange to be accorded the honorific of lady when one was not used to being addressed so. Henry sat back and admired her, the rose bloom still in her cheeks, the sparkle in her eyes, the animated smile as she answered his friend's questions finding humor in something he had said to her.

Henry heard only the answer. "I look forward to seeing all of my husband's estates if that is what he wishes me to do, but my first priority is the children. I feel children so young should be enjoying the country and not the more polluted air of London."

"Won't you miss the balls and entertainments? Where will you show off your gowns and the jewels I'm sure Hargrove will buy you."

"Oh, Lord Markham, I will find the country much more to my taste. I like to play outside in the garden with the children and spend my evenings reading aloud about dragons or pirates to them. I wouldn't know where to wear jewels, so I hope Henry doesn't bother buying me any."

His friend watched his wife closely as if trying to decide if her answers were genuine or contrived. "But haven't you lived in London these past years?"

"Yes, my entire life, although it isn't where I feel the most comfortable. First, my father then my husband needed to be in the city for business. They were both solicitors who needed to be near the courts and governmental buildings for filings and such."

"Strange, I never met a woman who didn't want the noise and glitter of a London season."

"Yes, my lord, but that may be because that is where you spend your time and so meet only women who are so inclined. Visit the country and you would probably come up with different views." The set down was gently done, and Henry felt pride that she hadn't backed down to allow Mark to feel vindicated in his ideas.

Henry could help pound the last nail into his friend's coffin. "I told you she was the woman who should have always been by my side. And the children love her."

Mark watched him closely. "I am not sure it is only the children, friend. But I apologize to the lady for assuming she didn't know what she wanted in this world. Playing with children on the grass and living in the country free of jewels. I stand corrected." He tipped his hat and sat back on the squabs.

Henry caught his friend's gaze and nodded accepting his friend's acceptance of Sarah. He didn't need the assurance, but he liked the fact Mark and Sarah may get along in the future. He would like to invite Mark out to the country estate once Sarah and his family were settled. He didn't foresee himself rushing back to London or its so-called merriment anytime soon.

They arrived at the Hargrove London house and

were met by the household staff in a long line of liveried servants and retainers, all smiling and wishing the newly married couple well. Sarah didn't need to be introduced since she was such a regular visitor, she had met them all at various times. The children were right inside the door holding the hands of their nurses. Mary dropped Lucy's hand to run toward Sarah.

"Oh, you're so pretty. Just like a princess. My mother would wear dresses like this, but I wasn't allowed to touch hers." The little girl had stopped abruptly when she reached the newly wedded couple.

"You may touch this one if you wish to because I want a hug from my new daughter."

"Me? Is it true then that I am your daughter in truth?"

"I am now your father's wife which makes me your mother, and I couldn't be happier, I truly couldn't." She hugged the girl to her, almost overwhelming the small body in the round skirt of her dress.

Henry picked Michael up and stood close to his daughter. "We are all a family now, Mary, and you can call her mother or mama if you like."

"I want her to be Mama since that is what she is to me. I always wanted someone to read to me and play with me like she does. I'll share her with Michael though because he needs a mama too."

Walking toward the formal dining room, Henry glanced over to Sarah saying, "That is very generous of you, Mary, but your mama is Michael's mama already. Your mama will be mama to all of my children."

Mary took a minute to digest this information before skipping into the room decorated with urns of flowers and candelabra burning brightly. The servants had turned the room into a veritable parkland and with the sun shining through the gleaming windows it resembled the gardens she imagined at the country estates.

It was a small party with Aggie saying she would dine with the other servants which left the small family, Lord Markham and the pastor of St. George's. There were a few toasts, many removes, and a traditional fruit cake for one of the desserts. Sarah was pleased with the show of kindness from the servants and from her husband who she was sure orchestrated some of the festivities.

"I am off to my club to be the first one to describe your lovely wife and this lovely event, Hargrove." Markham was holding his top hat and leaned toward his friend although Sarah heard his comment. "I believe you chose well this time without any advice from me. I would have snapped her up if I'd seen her first."

Henry said sotto voice while watching Sarah, "To be truthful, I think she was made for me. I don't know how I thought to go on without her."

She felt her cheeks warm as Markham turned to her and bowed over her hand once again. "My lady, best wishes to you until we meet again. I leave my best friend in your charge and care and expect to find him when next we meet as hale and hearty as he is now."

She smiled at this pure display of nonsense. "I shall do my best."

They stood together in the foyer alone for the first time as husband and wife. His brows rose in question. "Well, my lady wife, do we retire to the blue parlor and converse or retire to our individual sleeping chambers where I'm sure the skeptical Aggie is waiting for you?"

"Actually, Aggie likes you very much now that

you've won her over by sending me gifts and paying for her handsome uniforms as well as new boots and bonnet."

"I will do the same for you now that you're my wife. I can make the carriage available to take you to whatever shop you'd like tomorrow. We will remain in London for a few more weeks. Plenty of time to get dresses made and collected before we leave for the country."

"I would like to see to the children before they're put to bed. I know Michael was rather tired from missing his afternoon rest, but Mary will probably be awake and excited about our nuptials."

Smiling he responded, "I know what she feels like then for I am rather excited about our nuptials." She knew he teased her and wondered how close to the truth it came.

"I am cognizant of a man's needs, my lor…Henry. I would not deny you conjugal rights if I were able to fulfill my duty."

He stopped her, making her face him in the middle of the passageway. "That is exactly what I feared. You think it a duty. I wish you to think of it as a pleasant interlude. A harbor in the storm of life and way to ease your worry and share the burdens you may face. Making love is more than two bodies meeting and mating. I wish I could show you the difference between what I want to do and what you did with your husband." He seemed angry or rather frustrated with her.

"I'm sorry. I am trying to come to grips with the difference between the two of you, but I still worry you will find me wanting as he did. Then I will be facing another woman usurping my domain."

He pulled her into his arms. "Never. If I need to wait

years for you, I will, without ever thinking of breaking my vows. I promised you my wealth, my body today, and I'm not changing my mind. You'll decide when you're comfortable making the decision, and I will have to be patient."

She raised her head and tried to see his eyes in the dim light from the hallway sconces. "I am so blessed that you found me, so pleased you allowed me to mother Mary and Michael. I am the worse wife ever…"

"Don't ever think such a thing." Lowering his head, his lips covered hers. When she remained in his arms and didn't flinch away, he continued to apply pressure, move his lips across hers, and suck lightly on her lower lip before sliding his warm tongue into her mouth. She gasped at the erotic feel of him inside her body as he deepened the kiss.

They remained together, her tongue darting out to tease his and his response of putting a hand on her bottom to pull her hips closer to his. She could feel his erection and marveled that such a man as this one would find her remotely desirable although he must. Something drew him to her and, as plain as she thought herself, her new husband had different ideas as to her attraction.

Finally, with both of them breathing deeper, with her trying to sort out the myriad of feelings washing over and through her, he put her from him.

"If we're to see the children before they fall asleep, we need to stop this display of affection in the middle of the passageway. Not that I want to, but I pledged certain things to you when you accepted my proposal, and I don't intend to confuse you into making a precipitous decision."

"No, of course not. We wouldn't want to confuse

me…" She wasn't sure her legs could support her, although once she stepped away from him she found she could stand unaided and make her way to the children's rooms.

CHAPTER SEVEN

Henry checked the blue parlor knowing that was where he could normally find his wife at that time of night before going to her sleeping chamber and knocking lightly on the passageway door. He wouldn't use the door adjoining their rooms. Not until Sarah decided to make their marriage real. Aggie answered, a piece of lace in her hand.

"No, my lord, my lady isn't in her room. The baby's been a mite touchy these past two days due to his cuttin' teeth, and my lady is caring for him upstairs."

He knew he scowled saying, "That's what we have nursery maids for. If I wanted my wife to be awake all night and stuck away from me, I'd have made those arrangements." He stomped back down the hall and up the flight of steps to the next floor. A light showing under one of the doors to the nursery had him turn in that direction and open it slowly so as not to startle the occupants.

He was met with his wife's sleepy eyes as she waved him onto the cot next to her. "He's finally drifted off. He's in so much pain I hurt for him, poor poppet."

His anger and disappointment at not having her alone for conversation dissipated, and all he could see were two people whom he cared about tired and worn out. "How long will this last? You look tired, and where the hell is Lucy?"

"She was up with him all last night, so I told her to rest and I would rock him for a while. It's not as if we can make the pain go away, but it eases him when I hold him like this."

He watched his son's little mouth make sucking noises as he drooled onto the white cloth beneath his open lips. "Is there nothing that can be done? I don't remember this with Mary."

She continued in whispered tones. "It is much the same for all children, I am told. The nursemaid must have taken care of Mary during her teething."

He looked away. "I hadn't been as aware of my wife's failings with Mary as I was when Michael was born. I always stopped in when I was home each night, but often Mary was already in bed and asleep."

"That's not unusual for aristocratic parents. The rest of us must care for our own much of the time and know more about their lives. I don't remember having a nurse, but I did have a governess once I was eight or so." She patted Michael's back as he made a little whimpering noise which wrenched Henry's heart.

"Is there not anything to be done?"

"I gave him a rag with ice in it to chew on which seemed to help and rubbed oil of cloves on the reddened gums, but there isn't too much else. Not until they cut through and then we'll have our happy little Michael back."

"Growing up is hard no matter what the age. I remember getting leg cramps at school that brought tears to my eyes. I was told they were growing pains, but they were really quite relentless. Of course, I was growing inches per year which made my parents comment on my ability to outgrow both clothes and shoes each semester."

"We have that to look forward to then won't we. Perhaps I should order uniforms in several sizes at the start of each school term."

He laughed remembering those years and how long ago it was yet how short a time seemed to have passed. "I wouldn't want to live through those years again, but they weren't all bad. I met Markham there and others. Men who now sit with me in parliament, who argue with me and against me. Perhaps we should hold a dinner or ball before we leave for the country. I feel the need to repay people for entertainments I have attended—and to show off my wife."

She seemed to think about what he'd said. "A simple dinner wouldn't be out of the ordinary, but you must remember we are both in mourning even if most of the ton doesn't know that."

"You're right. Perhaps we should wait until we return from the country next year. Give time for people to become used to my remarrying so soon."

She lifted her head and gazed at him. "Have people said anything? Do they know about…"

"No, no, nothing like that. In fact, the ones who know about our marriage seem to think nothing of it and often give their own opinion about needing a mother for my two children. Since no one knows who you were or where you come from, I don't think there will be difficult questions asked."

"Good. I don't want anything to taint our family in any manner. Nothing for people to think about in the years to come."

He watched as her eyes almost closed. "Is he ready to be laid down yet? I could…"

"I plan on sleeping on that cot under you with him

next to me so I can comfort him if he wakens. I think he's almost through the worse of it, and he seems to settle easier with me right there when he wakes."

Standing, he peered longingly at the narrow mattress. "Wish I could convince you I needed comforting at night."

She gazed over to him. "I think that bed is a little too small for you at this point."

"But nestling into your bosom as Michael is sounds very appealing to me about now. I didn't know how difficult it was going to be to keep my promise when I made it that day in the garden."

"I'm sorry. There has been so much to do. Ordering clothes for myself and the children, figuring out which staff members will travel with us and who will remain in town. I haven't had time to think about more personal things…"

"I employ a steward to handle such things. Well, not your personal clothing, but everything else. Why isn't Stevens doing his job?" He was tired and cross and wanted her to himself.

"He is, husband, as well as explaining everything to me. I need to know what goes into such a move, and I am learning. It's simply that it takes time to get everything right."

He felt his bottom lip jut out like a petulant child's. "Stevens is very attractive, isn't he." A statement not a question. Even he who had never considered a man's attractiveness knew how the female house staff all swooned when the man is in the house.

"Yes, he is and much closer to my age than you are. That is where you were going with this line of questions wasn't it?" She wore an expression he had difficulty reading. She touched his arm. "Henry, if I cannot make up my mind whether I'm ready to bed my own husband, don't you think it a little precipitous of me to think about bedding anyone else?"

Feeling foolish for his unfounded jealousy, he snorted. "I can see you're tired and going to give me a difficult time. Come. Let me help you lie down with Michael and I'll be on my way."

She was smiling as she passed him to get to the edge of the bed, and he took advantage of her having her arms full of baby. Leaning down he covered her mouth as she raised her face to his as if expecting the salute.

"Good night, husband. I hope you feel better in the morning."

"Good night, wife. I already do." He left her reluctantly hoping she'd call him back, but silence filled the room behind him.

Tomorrow they would leave London and move to the country home closest to the city so Henry could make the trip by horse and return in one day. He said he would finish his duty in the House of Lords for the season before dedicating full-time to his wife and children. Sarah thought that once settled at Hargrove Court she would feel they could begin their married life. She learned through Aggie that Alicia had never spent any time in the country when Henry had and that the other woman refused to leave London no matter the season. Sarah would feel better sharing a bed with Henry if she needn't think he was comparing her to the last woman who was in that bed with him.

The move to the country took less time than Sarah had expected even travelling in a row of several coaches and wagons. She had known some personal items would go with them, but certain chairs and even paintings made the move as well. Packing them properly and storing them in the wagon without damage took days of preparation although the footmen and butler seemed well versed in doing the job. Sarah had spent the time getting the children prepared for the move.

She wanted the children with her in the coach and since, at the last minute, her husband told her he was travelling with her, she had dismissed the nursemaids to travel with Aggie and the valet in another carriage. She knew she could care for the children and hoped they were good travelers, but knowing Henry would be close gave her confidence the trip would go well for all of them.

As they pulled onto the highway and their coach towered over almost everything else on the road, she leaned back and expelled a deep breath.

"Was it that taxing?" her husband asked smiling.

"A little nerve racking is all. I wanted to make sure Ann Marie and Michael's lamb got into this coach and not packed away. If either one of those got misplaced it could have become a very difficult trip."

She glanced over to the doll and Mary who was sitting on her knees staring out the window taking in the London streets at their busiest as wagons, carts, and people made their way to the market areas from the seaports. Some cargo more odorous than others which smell worked its way into the otherwise pristine interior.

Michael sat on his father's lap, his dress covering his tiny shoes and his lace cap tied under his chin. She could see the similarities in the shape of their head, their mouth and eyes. She found herself softening toward her husband since she loved his son so deeply. She hadn't been aware of it occurring or even when the love deepened, but it was there, and she felt it toward both her men sitting next to her.

Michael rubbed his cheek against his father's coat and then his ear. Worried, Sarah leaned over to touch the reddened portion of his tiny body and felt her brows draw down in concern. "I think Michael may be getting an earache as well as cutting those back lower teeth. I hope he isn't in too much pain before we arrive and I can make willow bark tea."

"Perhaps he will sleep most of the way and not feel the pain."

The words were not out of the man's mouth before the baby whimpered and pulled at his ear, his sharp nails making marks on the tender skin. Sarah's heart ached knowing the pain he was suffering and reached out for him. Henry handed him over. His concerned expression made her realize how anxious he was over his son. She laid the bad ear against her breast hoping her body's warmth would sooth the toddler's distress. At least it would prevent the tyke from scratching at his ear.

The trip was broken midway for a meal and so everyone could walk the kinks out of their legs. Other than a quick visit to the facilities, Sarah remained holding Michael with Henry solicitously giving what aid and succor he could to his distressed son. And to his wife trying to relive that distress.

A fretting Michael was finally put to rest in his own cot carried by wagon from his room in London. A little more at ease, he settled for the night. Lucy had taken care to feed and wash Mary, and the little girl was now falling asleep in her own cot in her own room off the nursery.

Sarah gazed tiredly at her husband. "I didn't even get to see the house as we arrived. I'm sorry. I know you wanted to share your home with me, but Michael…"

"Do not think another thing about it. I was so grateful you were there to care for my son. He seems less restless in your arms than in anyone else's. It must be a mother's touch."

His words stirred something inside her, but she didn't argue. She couldn't feel more Michael's mother than if she had gone through the hours of labor to produce him. "I'm glad he feels I will be there for him. Earaches can be so painful for little ones." She now understood her husband's attitude that Mary was his true child no matter that another man had fathered her. The bond between two unrelated people, an adult and a child, blossoms into so much more so easily. They reach out with their little starfish hands and grab onto your heart.

Standing beside each other, they watched as sleep claimed the boy before turning away.

"I suppose you're going to stay with him to make sure he doesn't waken during the night in pain?"

"Yes, do you mind? I think what I saw of your house is beautiful, and the woodwork here in the nursery is lovely. The children are going to love sitting in the same chairs their father sat in as a child."

"If you move aside the curtains on that window, you'll see the initials I carved into the sill."

"Oh, you didn't do such a thing! Where was your nurse?"

"Probably sneaking kisses from one of the footmen in the hallway. I remember seeing them slip out the door and knew I would have plenty of time to do most anything I wanted while she was busy."

"Well, I don't think Lucy or Mavis would do such a thing." She shook her head muttering, "Anything could have happened."

"I'm sure many things were happening in the hallway that I was unaware of at the time, but I never came to any harm in here alone. Surrounded by my toy soldiers and rocking-horse…"

She laughed quietly. "You sound as if you have pleasant memories of this room."

"Yes, my cousins would come to visit, and we would build tents inside and forts outside. We had good times, but life goes on. They married and had families of their own. We grew apart since Alicia hated the country and wouldn't think of holding a house party so far out of town."

She cocked her head. "Is that what you'd like? For us to hold a house party and invite those same cousins along with their families for an extended stay?"

He became quiet and then smiled, nodding. "Yes, I think that would be a wonderful time. Their children will get to know ours, and I can show off my wife and all her wonderful womanly attributes. I would love to reconnect with them and see how well they are getting on."

"As soon as we can manage it, I'll talk with the housekeeper here and see how many rooms could be made ready. Then send out the invitations."

He leaned over and kissed her lips quickly before pulling away, his arms crossed over his chest. "I look forward to their visit. I'll make up a list of names as soon as my office is unpacked."

"How are my girls this morning?" Henry said entering the nursery and finding only Mary and Sarah sitting on the carpet holding a sleeping Michael. His wife appeared tired with dark smudges beneath her eyes, but she answered happily.

"We are planning a picnic outside now that the sun has promised to shine today. With Michael so fussy I'm afraid Mary has had to forego any outings, but he is much happier this morning after his tooth cut through. I even have the little gnaw marks on my finger to prove it."

"Then it sounds as if you both deserve a special treat. How about I join you, and we will all ride down to the river in the pony cart?"

He knew Mary loved the old pony used to pull the ramshackle farm cart so hoped her enthusiasm would cloak the real reason for his asking to be included. He had spent several hours last night thinking about his wife, thinking about her in that small cot when she could be sharing his expansive mattress. This waiting was proving taxing on his body and his nerves.

He spent too much time wondering if today would be the day his wife felt comfortable enough to join him—literally. And if he weren't tortured enough during his waking hours his dreams made his need ten times stronger. Since being married to Sarah, his mind often took over his sleep, and he spent hours rolling on his mattress in feigned ecstasy only to wake unfulfilled and aching. Some body parts were not made to be teased for long periods of time.

Even now, watching her gently stroke Michael's hair could bring a rise to certain body parts left unmentioned although very much on his conscience.

Mary jumped up interrupting his imaginings. "Can we go now, Papa? I can get my doll and be ready as soon as Lucy gets back."

"And where did the estimable Lucy go?"

Sarah answered. "She is picking up the clean laundry and telling Cook we will need a selection of her best items for our picnic."

"Sounds as if she has an estimable duty to perform. I, too, will need to cover a few things with my steward and then change for a day with my family." He glanced at his wife, but found her smiling without sign she didn't want him along. In fact, he thought she appeared quite pleased with his plans.

Sarah watched her husband of three weeks pat his daughter on the head as he passed her to change clothes. How had she ever gotten so lucky as to have caught his eye? Hadn't he seen the grey hairs that already showed on her head? Hadn't he realized it portended the silvery hair of her father so early in his life? Or the clothes she wore which were little better than those bought from the consignment shop? Even her wedding dress had been one found at the last minute. Aggie and her daughter worked on it diligently so it was ready in time for the hastened wedding.

Henry never found anything to criticize although there was ample to critique if he were of a mind. Unlike Richard who often commented negatively on her dress style. Sarah never pointed out that fashion cost money, and he had told her many times that costs must be kept as low as possible until he gained recognition in his field. While all the time spending money on keeping the house on Curzon Street and his mistress in jewels.

And Henry had been correct in saying that running his household would be easy due to the fine quality of servants and their long standing in his house. They had all been welcoming, and no one had criticized her attempts at anything. They all seemed to be pleased she was trying and gave her every suggestion and advice to help her along the way. Any fear of not being able to run a large household had evaporated.

Now she would face a large gathering as hostess. A gathering of people who had not visited this home in decades. She would need to pull resources she hadn't used since before her father died. She had done it then, mingling with judges as well as other governmental dignitaries, and she could do it again. Only in a grander scale and without the budget restrictions she had to follow with her father's limited income.

If she had known that her sacrifices during her first marriage had been paying for Richard's lover's little extras, she would have spent every penny she could get her hands on and then some.

She leaned down and kissed Michael's hair and chided herself. No, she wouldn't waste time or thoughts on what was in the past. It was dead and buried, and she should concentrate on what life had given her. The blessings of being the mother to these two darling children. Children not of her blood or body but so precious she thanked God for them daily.

And she could have even more blessings if she could find it in her heart to trust Henry and his promise of faithfulness. She wouldn't demand love or even fake moments of attentiveness. Merely the vow of not humiliating her and making her feel as if she should be a woman to pity.

Sarah was beginning to believe her new husband and his promises even after the last one had deceived her so thoroughly. Henry was a wonderful father taking time to see his children each evening, listening to her read quietly and then kissing them goodnight. She had watched Henry wipe the drool from his son's painful gums and try to sooth him when he cried. What other father of his standing did such things?

Lucy returned and gathered a few toys and wraps in case the day became chilly nearer the water. Sarah told the girl since Lord Hargrove was going along, that the nursemaids could have the afternoon to themselves. Wearing a simple dress several years old, she told Aggie her plans on the way down to the foyer and accepted a bonnet and shawl from her as well.

"All ready?" her husband asked as a footman tried to help carry the items Lucy felt necessary plus the toys Mary thought she and Michael would need.

Sarah answered, "Yes, but I didn't imagine this outing would mean so much chaos."

"Nothing we can't handle." Gazing up at his face glowing with health and happiness she had to agree. Everything probably did magically go right when he wished it to. He could enchant a recent widow, unhappy with marriage in general, and have her remarried within a month of her husband's funeral. This man could do anything he said he would. This man's word was a solemn vow.

They piled into the farm cart which showed its age and creaked with the loading of each item. The placid pony with its long eyelashes stood sedately as commotion erupted on all sides of him. Henry sat a now wide-awake Michael on the horse's back and held him in place as the footmen loaded the cart and put folded blankets so the occupants could sit comfortably. It appeared Henry would be driving the lone animal as he settled Michael onto Sarah's lap and took the reins.

"Hold on as we're off to the river. I had fishing poles added to the necessities," Henry announced over his shoulder.

Sarah peered about her and laughed at her imagining it would be Lucy, her, and the two children with a basket walking to the farthest corner of the garden.

The cart lumbered over the uneven ground once they left the drive toward a stand of trees winding their way behind undulating hills of grass. It finally came to a stop, and Mary squealed to be lifted down.

"Stay right next to the cart, Mary. I don't want to need to fish you out of the water," she warned.

"Oh, Mama, I know better than to fall into the river."

Sarah's breath caught, and her eyes misted over—the first time Mary had called her Mama. Her gaze met Henry as he took Michael from her lap to allow her to disembark over the rear gate. The feelings Mary's words had evoked were too much, too fresh for her not to react emotionally. She held out her arms for Michael, and Henry placed him back into them.

"I taught Mary to swim last summer so she'll not come to any harm. She knows the rules to wait for me until I can be beside her when she approaches any form of water."

Sarah smiled and nodded. "That's very good, then. I think everyone should learn to swim when they are young. Perhaps when we have the family for a visit, if the weather is still warm, we can have a picnic here for all of us."

"If not a picnic, then we men will come down to fish. I have a collection of reels for casting for trout that need to be used."

She raised an eyebrow. "Then I will put fishing on the list for either sex to participate in. It is not only men who enjoy casting a fly now and then."

His brows rose in surprise. "So, do you wish to place

a bet on which one of us catches the largest fish?"

She lifted her chin at the dare. "Of course, what shall be the wager?"

He stopped lifting the basket out of the cart, and his gaze focused on her lips. "I'll take a kiss as my reward."

She smiled and turned away saying, "Isn't that like a prize to the loser, as well?"

He caught up with her and spread the blanket where she indicated allowing the branches to shade most of it to keep Michael from getting sunburned. She finally built up the courage to glance at her husband, and he was still grinning, glancing in her direction as he laid out the children's belongings along the edge of the blanket.

Mary was gathering wild flowers close to where the pony had been tethered so they were alone with their conversation.

"So, there is hope for us then?" he asked trying to get her attention.

She kept her head turned blocking her face with the brim of her sun hat. "I don't know what you mean. Why wouldn't there be hope?"

"I was beginning to wonder. I know I promised to give you time, but it seems if we are not talking about the children, we aren't talking at all. Your comment gave me hope."

She felt it time to be as honest with him as she had been trying to be with herself. "Yes, there is hope, and I will give you an answer very soon."

His serious expression disappeared as he laughed. "Good, but that doesn't mean I won't claim my prize if I hook the largest fish."

She allowed Mary to hold her pole with the line in the water and pointed out how the bobber would disappear if a fish took the hook. Henry had a casting rod for himself which she knew gave him a better advantage, but didn't think giving him a kiss was any hardship on her part. "Mary, let me know if you have even a nibble."

A moment later the little girl was shaking with excitement calling out, "Papa, Papa, come quick. I think I've got one."

He walked down the bank toward his daughter and laid his pole down to help her hold hers. There was a fish on the end of the line, and he helped her pull it in to shore where he reached down and lifted the flopping trout by the line.

"That's a good-looking fish, Mary. Your first one ever." Her father's compliment made the girl stand taller as she watched the fish lie on the river's bank.

"It's huge isn't it, Mama?" The girl was laughing in glee. "Can we eat it?"

Sarah laughed with her daughter. "We can have the cook fry it for you, Darling. I'm sure she won't mind."

She shared a rueful look with her husband. "This seems likely the only fish being caught today, and neither of us caught it."

"I can share, Mama."

"I know you will, Poppet, but your father and I had a bet which appears to be null and void. It's time to get out the picnic and eat our meal," she answered still watching her husband's noncommittal expression.

They placed the fish in the river on a stringer, washed their hands, and picked up the poles on their way back to the blanket. Sarah began unpacking the food and crock of lemonade which still felt cool before pouring it into three glasses balanced in the grass.

The meal was exactly what the children liked to eat

with some adult provisions as well. They ate more than they would have if sitting at a table, and soon Michael showed signs of wanting his cot again.

Henry began packing up. "Sarah, please take care of the children while I pack up and wake up the pony. I heard him snoring while we were eating."

"Really, or are you merely teasing Mary and me?"

"No, this old hack tends to nap during the heat of the day and probably more often than that. I don't blame him, I'd like a rest about now, too." He continued to pick up items, tossing them into the basket brought down from the nursery.

She watched him move easily between the ground and the basket while she made sure Mary had her doll and Michael his lamb. She helped Henry get both settled in the blankets before climbing in next to them. The horse was turned around, and the jerky ride home began.

CHAPTER EIGHT

Sarah looked herself in the eyes in the mirror's reflection. She could do this. She could be Henry's wife in all ways. She could go to his room and tell him she was ready.

Any feeling of strength wilted as she took in her simple night rail, her long auburn braid plaited to one side, and her bare feet. She didn't own a pair of slippers since she never found a need for them before. Usually, she woke each morning and dressed immediately for her day of work. Lounging around wearing house slippers had never been part of her life.

Inhaling, she nodded at the woman facing her and pulled on her worn wrapper tying it tightly as if for protection. She needed to stop that. She needed Henry to be the husband she thought he would be. She needed to trust.

Walking down the hallway rather than knocking at the adjoining door seemed right. This way if he denied her entrance or if the valet were still with him, she could say something about the children and leave. Save face and then go back to her room and die of humiliation. Could there be anything more embarrassing then to find the room empty or occupied only by the valet?

She tapped lightly thinking the room must be empty due to the lack of light shining under the door. As she turned, the door opened and Henry stood there a smile curving his attractive mouth up at each corner.

"I thought I heard someone out here. Would you care to come in?"

No need to explain why she was there. He stepped back and welcomed her inside. Her gaze travelled over the room. It had wood paneled walls with coffered ceiling and dark draperies. It appeared more as a library or office would rather than a sleeping chamber. The door to the dressing room and bath were closed but their placement was the mirror image of her room.

A heavy brocade cover was pushed back and the bed open for him. He was dressed much as she was with his bare chest showing at the open collar of his banyan tied closed. He was wearing slippers, and she covered one foot with the other to hide her toes. The high poster bed was intimidating, and he must have seen that fear because he stepped toward her with his hand out and open palmed.

"Sarah, don't lose your nerve now that you've gotten here. I can't be so frightening you would turn from me after finally coming this far."

She knew he didn't mean in feet, but in their relationship, in her journey of becoming his wife, a woman who shared her husband's bed. "I, ah, I came to pay you for losing the wager. I didn't catch the largest fish."

"Dressed as you are, can I hope you're here for more?" He kept a few feet from her but remained between her and the door.

"I thought so. I mean, I think I'm ready for more…"

She nodded and felt his arms around her body as she raised her head to accept his kiss. As soon as their lips touched, she knew she had chosen the right path. Knew that she not only trusted him, but felt a stronger emotional connection to him, more than anything she had ever felt for her late husband.

That was the last time she wanted to think about Richard. About her failure in her marriage, about her failure to keep her husband satisfied and at home. Tonight was for her and Henry, and she was going to allow herself to enjoy this new relationship, possibly add to their family and learn to love her new life.

"That was in payment of the wager," he explained teasingly. "My hands were on the fishing pole when the trout was brought to shore."

He hesitated and seemed to think about what he was going to say, how he wanted to word things. "Sarah, your first marriage didn't seem to be very good for you, and I understand this would make you skittish, but part of any relationship is trust. I trust you to keep to your vows, and I want you to trust me to do the same and not hurt you in any way."

"I-I never conceived during the years I was married…" She spoke so quietly he had to turn his good ear toward her. "It is difficult to remind you I may be barren, may not be able to give you the large family you seem to want, but I am willing to try."

"Did you participate in trying to have a child? Did your husband spend much time in your bed?" He asked it so matter-of-fact that she answered easily without thinking it a strange question to answer.

She knew he meant while spending time with Alicia had Richard spent any time in her bed. "Of course, my husband visited my bed at least once a week, well most of the time, a little less for the past year or so." She knew her brows drew down as she thought back to the last time he had visited her bed with any regularity. "I guess it was becoming less and less, but when we were first married, he was very regular—every Wednesday except for the week of my, um-m-m, when I was unavailable."

"Alicia spent Wednesday evenings with a group of women friends so that would leave him at loose ends." He seemed to gaze pityingly. "Your brief times together could account for you never getting with child."

"I don't understand. We were married doing, ah, doing married things." She searched her mind for any reason that made it difficult for her to conceive.

"The more often one has marital congress the more likely of conception to occur. I plan on us being very busy together, and hopefully we will get the results we want. That is for you to have a child from your womb and for me to have a content wife." He explained as if she were a small child uncomprehending of the facts of life. But she had been a married woman for two years, and she knew about marriage. Still Henry sounded as if he knew about such things and he had fathered a child, so perhaps she should acquiesce to his greater knowledge.

"I will try to be a wife to you and hope the outcome will bring us a child."

He dropped his robe and turned toward her. His naked body showed he was more than pleased to see her. He must have noticed her eyes enlarge as she stepped back from him.

He seemed confused by her hesitation and put his robe back on. "I won't hurt you."

She knew her voice trembled. Now that she was this far into her plan, she was beginning to worry whether she could follow through with it. "It always hurts."

His brows drew down. "It always…what do you mean? Your husband hurt you when you were intimate?"

"Yes, but he said he couldn't do anything about it. It's not like he hit me or anything. It simply hurt."

He moved closer, and she stayed her ground willing to allow him access to her body. She wanted to be with him like this. Wanted to feel his weight on her. Wanted to know what being with him was like.

"Did you ever see anyone about it? Have a physician examine you?"

"Yes, but the doctor never actually examined me, I mean, down there." She felt as if her face were burning with the heat of her mortification. How had she allowed this conversation to get to this point? "He told me I would become accustomed to my husband given time. He didn't say how long that would take so I never spoke of it again."

"I can assure you, it shouldn't hurt in any way. Let me make love to you, and I'll show you how it can be good between a man and a woman."

"I heard women say how much they enjoyed being with men, and the affair my husband had proved he wasn't at fault."

"It doesn't prove you were at fault either. Sometimes men don't take the time required to ensure their partner is readied to receive them."

She wasn't sure she understood. It was like listening to someone speak a foreign language. "I don't think I understand, although I do wish to lie with you. I have found myself thinking of you and having strange yearnings to be near you, to join with you. I want a child, to feel my body get big and to nurture that infant. I won't mind the pain."

He reached out for her and pulled her to his chest. "There will be no pain if I do things correctly. I always thought trust is a prerequisite between couples. Do you trust me?"

"I can stand it for however long it takes to conceive a child." She saw him wince as she spoke.

He moved to pull her to his chest, and she flinched before calming herself to accept his touch. "Sarah, I will never hurt you."

"I agree you would never mean to hurt me. I trust you to be faithful and to care for me and the children forever."

He reached for her again. "I want you to trust me and trust that I know what I'm doing."

Accepting his hand, she allowed him to lay her onto the bed where he climbed next to her leaving his slippers on the floor. Leaning over her, he kissed her mouth several times, sucking her bottom lip and licking with his tongue until she opened her mouth in an erotic gasp.

Her breath caught at the sensation shooting through her body and going straight between her legs. She couldn't take time to analyze what was happening to her as he continued kissing a trail back to her mouth.

She smiled but was too interested in what he was doing to her mouth to argue over the rules of the wager. Responding to his insistent tongue, she dueled with it liking the sensation of its warmth sliding over her lips and tongue. His head lowered and followed a trail down to the tender spot under her ear and then pushed at her neckline sprinkling kisses around her night rail's collar.

Stretching her neck to give him more access, he untied the wrapper's belt and let it fall open. He loosened the ribbon holding the round neckline closed giving him freedom to the rest of her neck and shoulder, which he sucked lightly, making her squirm with need for more.

More of what, she wasn't sure, but she knew Henry understood, trusted Henry to assuage her need for more. And he did. He pushed the sleeves and night rail down her arms to her waist. She felt the cooler air against her burning skin and then the warmth of his mouth covering one nipple.

Arching into him, her hands held his head in position not wanting him to leave while at the same time silently begging him to do the same to the other breast. She didn't know how much more of this she could stand. Soon his mouth left her breast and traveled down her body, the clothing shoved to her ankles without thought.

He kissed her stomach, and she felt the urge to curl her legs up and cover that part of her body, but remembered in time she had said she would allow him access to her, to her body, to her womanhood. She wanted a child, and this man was the only way to having one of her very own from her so far empty womb.

"Henry! What do you think you're doing?" She suddenly startled at where he was kissing her.

"I know what I'm doing, and you told me you trusted me. Now show me that you do. Relax and just feel…"

Unsure if she could relax with his mouth over her most private part, she felt his tongue enter her. It felt cool to her heated body, and the movements imitated what he had done to her mouth a few minutes earlier. Clenching her fists around the sheet, she tried to do as he had said. Relax and trust—but it was stretching her ability to remain still. She was used to lying perfectly quiet while her husband had his pleasure, but this was becoming more difficult as Henry continued teasing body parts she never knew she had before. Teasing her into writhing to escape the sensations building to something she didn't understand.

"Henry, please, I can't take any more."

He held her hips with his body and covered her breast with one hand. The other was stroking deeply into her, and she was unable to control a violent burst of sensations uncoiling from deep inside and travelling to the tips of her toes and fingers. She arched into him as the phenomenon burst upon her and he held her tightly. Fireworks went off behind her eyelids, and she thought she would explode into a million pieces before it was all over.

His breath blew over the hair on her mound and she again wanted to escape this bed, this man, but remained unmoving. A shudder ran through her body when his fingers again gently touched her there. Not that she hadn't been touched there although not with this intensity. Usually, to make sure the positioning was right before Richard entered her. Before Richard rutted within her and then left to sleep in his own room afterward.

Henry touched deeper inside her than anyone ever had, and she couldn't hold back the whimper of fear escaping.

"Sh-h-h-h, Sweeting, I promise not to hurt you. Trust me in this."

She nodded, biting her lip hoping not to show fear of this sort of intimacy. Especially not after the pleasure he had just given her. Her promise to herself was surely tried when she felt the warmth of his tongue replace his fingers and the mingling of his breath on the intimate area that was beginning to feel it belonged to him as much as it did to her.

Positioning his chest between her legs, he nudged them apart and she felt unsure of what to do, what to say when a man was so busy between one's thighs, how to go on or where to place one's hands. And what to say when the sensations began rolling through her body again. Sensations that swirled up from deep down and rose to the surface. At least the surface the size of a pinpoint at the center of his attention.

Following a gentle sucking, her body suddenly bucked and writhed trying to escape the intense feeling much stronger than the first. Sarah gripped the sheet in both hands pushing down with her hips. Henry lifted her buttocks with his hands and sucked harder bringing a long keening from deep in her throat. Although she was embarrassed by the sounds being drawn from her, he chuckled and increased his attentions. She felt herself tighten and tighten until she broke apart into what felt like shards of glass flying over the entire room and then came back together as Henry climbed to her side.

Her husband chuckled again. "I pronounce you completely fit to make love and try for a child of your own."

Henry held her and stroked down her side, slowly kissing her temple. "I assume that was your first orgasm? I hope you enjoyed this as much as I did pleasuring you."

"I never...I didn't understand what it was all about." She couldn't catch her breath, make sense of her body's response. "An orgasm? It was so—so amazing. How can I ever thank you?"

When she finally thought herself calmed, she said, "You know I love both of the children. This isn't to replace them, but I need to know I can do the basic duty of a woman. I need to know that my not having a child wasn't the cause for Richard leaving me, going to a woman who had proven fertile, who had already given him a child."

"Darling, you must remember, Richard had already been in a relationship with Alicia for years before he married you. Having a child already may have lessened his need to have one with you. I think the man was simply selfish and never thought about you or your needs. Too many men are raised that way and think only of their own release. Let me touch you freely, and I can show you what can be had between a man and a woman."

She thought they must be past that but nodded, wondering what more he could do to her, with her, that would equal or surpass what she had barely lived through already.

Shrugging out of his robe left him naked next to her, and she reached over to hold him intimately, show him she had no fear of him any longer and that she wanted to give him pleasure. He moaned and pressed into her palm.

His hand cupped one bare breast and brought the nipple to a hard peak again using just his bare palm. The other nipple he covered with his mouth, his tongue flicking the tip while suckling as she imagined an infant would.

His mouth returned to cover hers, his tongue seeking entry while one hand smoothed over a breast. He continued to kiss her mouth before moving across her jaw and onto her neck which made her raise her shoulders since it tickled. He made little sucking noises bringing a smile to her face as she felt him continue a path down her body spending a little time suckling each pebbled nipple.

"I have something in mind, and I hope you'll enjoy it as much as I will. Is there still trust between us?"

"Of course, I want to give you as much pleasure as you've given me." She felt as if he had been doing all the giving while she had remained passive. Perhaps that part of her lovemaking wasn't correct either.

"Don't worry, I'll make sure we both enjoy ourselves."

He kissed her, pulling her under his body and entwining his legs with hers. Teasing the nubs on each breast, her body responded as it had previously, and she felt warm and moist between her legs. This time the tightening of muscles was not surprising, the coiling of want anticipated as it tightened deep inside.

This time Henry stayed kissing her mouth and nudged her legs apart which she let move easily as he nestled between her thighs. She felt his firm staff at her entrance and geared herself to lie and not flinch when the pain came. Closing her eyes, she tensed waiting for the pain.

He pushed into her then stopped moving, lying there kissing her mouth gently. "Are you feeling any pain?" At the shaking of her head, he sighed pressing down once again.

She was filled with his firm male part, smooth and touching every fiber of her body that responded to its touch. Her internal muscles clenched in reaction to the pleasure once again as she rose to meet him. "Um-m-m, it feels wonderful."

A deep, sexy chuckle rumbled through his chest as he bent to nuzzle her neck. "You know what a man wants to hear from his partner…"

He began to slide out and she pulled his buttocks

toward her unwilling to let him leave her now but she hadn't needed to. He thrusted in again and prepared to pull back while holding her hips to his body urging her to rock with him.

She wrapped her legs around him to ensure he was imbedded as deeply as possible which seemed to please him. He increased speed while kissing her several times in a row. A low growl escaped him as his hand flexed to lift her with him. She realized, unlike her late husband, Henry wanted her to move, seemed to want her to enjoy the joining with him.

She met his thrusts and felt the coil peak and then spin out to the tips of her body once more. Her hips raised off the mattress meeting his hips as he too tensed feeling his seed enter her womb. This, this must mean she would get with child. How could anything this marvelous, this passionate not create a child?

His thrusts continued hard and fast. She wrapped her arms around him as he pumped deeper and her body tensed waiting for the final relief. Soaring with the heady release of another orgasm she floated back to the mattress trying to catch her breath. Henry lay panting on her, his arms holding as much of his weight off her although they remained joined. She flexed her internal muscles, and he responded with a groan into her neck.

He kissed her temple between taking deep gulping breaths and calming her as he had earlier. "No pain, I hope. Are you still happy you asked me to make love to you?"

"Yes, and I'm sure I'll see myself with a child soon."

"I hope not too soon. I don't want to consign us to sleeping alone."

"Is that how it's done? We must no longer do this once I'm with child?"

The questions must have made him contemplate possibilities as he said slowly, "No, I don't think there's any reason to stop making love, not until the very last weeks if there isn't a problem. If you wish to sleep with me then I certainly won't complain."

"I think as long as the doctor doesn't warn against it, we will do so."

She was rewarded with a hug and deep kiss from the man whom she would always think of as her husband from this moment on. The father of her future child when she once had thought she would never have a child from her own body. She loved Mary and Michael, of course, but the maternal need of bearing a baby was strong.

Henry woke her two more times in the middle of the night, ending up with making love in a different manner each time telling her both times that it would be the last for the night. That he wanted to make sure she was all right and that making love hadn't hurt in any manner. By morning she wasn't sure her answer was the same any longer.

He was up and beginning to dress himself when she finally opened her eyes to daylight. He sat on the edge of the bed and stroked her through the sheet bringing heat to her cheeks. "I rang for Aggie and told her to bring up a warm bath. It sounds as if she's about done, and Jason has been hovering in the hallway. I suggest you use the adjoining door this time—and from now on, or I can go to your room. I'm comfortable either way."

She was glad he meant to continue as they were going. After last night and learning about what a marriage consisted of between the husband and wife, she wanted to keep sleeping with her husband. She felt she would miss his touch and his warmth if she returned to sleeping alone as she had always done.

"I will take that suggestion. Um-m, do you know where my robe is?"

"Certainly, allow me to help you on with it. Where are your slippers?"

"I don't have any."

He gazed into her eyes. "No matter. I don't foresee you running back and forth anyway. I can do that part."

"Thank you." She wished she could stay, wished they had more time together, but their lives were already pulling them apart.

Reaching the door, she found it unlocked. Before she could open it, she heard her name called. Turning back to him, she found his expression impossible to read. "I'll see you at breakfast as usual, and I plan to spend the day with you and the children again."

She held the promise close to her heart and entered her room finding Aggie there placing towels and soap within reach of the tub.

Embarrassed, Sarah said nothing, but dropped the robe on the seat of a chair.

"About time I'd say, my lady. That man was as antsy as a fly in a room full of horse tails."

"Who? Lord Hargrove?"

"Yes, his lordship. The man has been watching you like a moonstruck lad although maybe no one else noticed, 'cept people never see servants and I'm the closest one to you."

"Oh, Aggie, you must be wrong because my husband and I had an agreement. I finally decided I had nothing to fear and everything to gain. I want a child that

I can give birth to, feed from my body, and know every moment of its life. I want to be a mother from the very start."

"That ain't a bad wish, my lady, but I seen you with those babes, and you're a mother already even if you didn't give them life. You're makin' their lives worth living, and that is as good if not better." Agatha put away the robe and straightened the jars on the dressing table. "Giving birth don't make a woman a mother, you know. I heard words about that first wife of his, and she weren't a mother, not at all."

"Aggie, please don't gossip about the children's mother. I don't want their feelings hurt when they get old enough to understand what they might hear now."

"I understand, my lady. It's just as I says. You're already their mother in all ways that matters."

She smiled and giggled as she sank into the warm water. "And I'm a wife now, too, so I feel all is right in my world."

At breakfast she found a less than happy husband eating a plate of ham and eggs with a side of kippers. He stood and smiled as she entered. After being seated, she heard him order her a huge breakfast, but didn't contradict him since she was famished. But how had he known that?

Sitting next to her, he handed her a piece of toasted bread spread with marmalade. "I received a packet from the House of Lords. The vote has been pushed forward, and we need every vote we can get or the fools will have the common people rioting in the streets. Prices must go down and taxes, too. No one will be able to afford bread if this continues."

She was disappointed, but tried not to show it. "I'll

explain to Mary, and little Michael doesn't understand you were going to be with them again anyway. What can I do to help things along while you are gone?"

"Be my countess and take care of our children. If neighbors call, have Bates or Stevens send them away. Tell them I'm in London and will accept visitors when I return."

"Oh, I couldn't do that. It seems rude." Then she thought about things. "Or are you afraid I'll say something gauche and not know how to go on."

"You would be fine with anyone visiting from around here. I merely thought you would want me here to introduce you to our neighbors. All of whom are beneath you in rank and station. The highest title we have here is the squire who has been knighted and a Baron who owns a milk farm a few miles from here."

She gazed into his eyes. "Are you sure you're not afraid I'll embarrass you? I could keep out of sight if you think it best."

He huffed a long breath out and waited for her plate to be placed in front of her and the footman to leave. "I think you are amazing, and anyone meeting you will realize what a lucky man I am to have found the perfect mate."

She laughed. "Now, my lord, you are doing it up too brown. I will try to wait for your return, but if it appears as if I am hiding, I feel I must meet them."

"I want you to feel comfortable, so do whatever you feel is best." He stuffed two bites of eggs into his mouth and picked up a piece of crisp bacon to go. "I must rush to reach town in time to place my vote. I don't know why people can't simply write in their vote and save all this running back and forth."

Wiping his mouth with the napkin he threw it onto his plate. Leaning down, he kissed her smack on the mouth then whispered, "Don't worry about anything. I will be back and continue as we did last night. I want to make sure you remember I'm your husband and mean to keep you in my bed as much as possible. If they don't handle this vote in a quick manner, I'll return to you and the rest can go hang."

She watched as her frustrated husband rushed out, the valet meeting him outside the door with a small valise of clothes, she was sure. She ate everything on her plate and wiped her mouth of any possible crumbs or damning smears. Standing, she made way to the children's rooms, but not before telling the butler she would like to speak with the steward when he was available.

The first visitors arrived by carriage. Since Sarah had been caught walking beside the children after picking wildflowers in the fallow field, she felt she had to invite the squire and his wife in for tea. Handing the tired children to Lucy and Mavis, Sarah ignored the stems and leaves decorating the hem of her skirts and led the couple into the family parlor. Bates was right behind her so she could give orders for tea to be brought.

The squire was a robust man and his wife almost as much so. His face was florid and his nose showed veins indicating he might drink a bit. His wife was rather loud and boisterous and neither were intimidating which Sarah was very thankful for.

After the tea arrived and Sarah poured, the squire's wife got down to the real reason for their visit. "We met the first wife, the one who died recently, when we were in London a few years back. Thought to visit the lord and his lady once we were in town to be neighborly. She barely stopped to say a hello before she excused herself to go shopping. I thought shopping could have waited since we had come all that way."

"Now Bess, the lady explained she had an appointment, and appointments must be kept. It's not as if she knew we'd be coming." He accepted a macaroon from the plate Sarah offered him.

"I realize that, but in town things are different. There are set times for visits, and we were there within the set time." The squire's wife showed her offended sensibilities still, and Sarah felt the woman had been hurt by the first countess's lack of concern.

"I plan on being in the country often so I shall make time to invite you both for dinner. That is once Lord Hargrove's responsibilities to the House of Lords is complete for this session."

"Ah, yes, I always thought Hargrove a good chap to place his votes where we need them. Not that it always goes our way, but at least he's trying. There are many others who ignore their duty. It's a shame." His wife nodded in agreement as she placed another macaroon in her own mouth.

Since Sarah wasn't sure exactly how often and when her husband voted she kept quiet. This was a lack of knowledge she wasn't comfortable with and thought to talk to the steward or Henry himself as soon as possible. She continued to smile, agreed that she should attend the local parish church since the living was given by Lord Hargrove and admitted she should know the pastor there. Sarah said she would consider whether she would have time to help with the annual Mayfair market next spring explaining she wasn't sure when the family would need to return to London.

As her guests were led out of the parlor by the butler, she felt exhausted. No wonder Henry suggested she not be at home when visitors cropped up. She felt as if she had run a mile, and it wasn't even afternoon yet.

She changed from her earlier gown, ate a light meal with the children, and then left to find the steward when the little ones lay down for their daily rest. Bates accompanied her to the steward's office and announced her to Stevens as if they had never met.

The handsome man bowed, and she remembered how jealous Henry seemed when he thought she was seeing this man too often. "My lady, how can I be of service? Please do not tell me we are moving back to town already." He laughed knowing she wouldn't want to accomplish that feat again so soon either.

"No, I hope this won't be as onerous. Lord Hargrove mentioned having his family come for a house party. He told me he had lost track of them as they grew into adulthood, but wishes to reconnect, meet their children, you know such things as that."

"It sounds as if my lord is beginning to live a more normal life. It will be good to see this house and the master come alive again." It seemed as if he caught himself and added, "Begging your pardon, my lady, I meant no offense, but I knew him before and after his marriage. The first one, I mean, and the change…I mean to say…"

Placing a hand up to stop his embarrassed apology, she said, "No need to explain, Stevens. It is good you think of Henry so personally that you worry about his happiness as well as his assets and estates."

"Thank you, my lady. I am glad he seems to want to do more. Getting back out to the country is the main thing even if he must return to London for the House of Lords and all."

"Henry said he'd give me a list of names for the invitations and, after I've talked with you and the butler and housekeeper, I plan to select a date for the event. Then I can figure out the menu with cook, the rooms with the housekeeper, the stable master for…"

"My lady, you needn't do everything. I will figure out the need of stable room and extra feed for the cattle. I will also make room for the grooms and drivers that will attend those guests arriving with their own equipage. The housekeeper will find rooms for the ladies' maids and any other indoor servants who may be coming."

"I hadn't thought about the grooms and possible outriders. I guess we must make a list and begin as soon as we can making arrangements."

"Much depends on how many will accept the invitation, my lady. I know we send regards each year, but I do not know their ages and if they are well enough to travel. Other than Lord Markham, no one else has ever accompanied Lord Hargrove here besides Lady Mary, of course."

"Does that mean you have the list of his relatives? At least that would give me a general idea of how many we are talking about. I'm not even sure how many rooms are available for occupation."

"Fifteen sleeping chambers, five suites with two bedrooms each, and two dormitory style rooms with six beds each for the unmarried adult members, if there are any. And, of course, there is an extra two rooms in the nursery section. Over two dozen servants' quarters before we need to start doubling-up which in the old days happened all the time. Being so close to London, this estate became a favorite with my lord's father and grandfather."

"Oh, that sounds like a lot of people. Perhaps Henry won't want to invite all of them or they won't all be able to attend."

"That's the rooms we have, my lady. I take very good care of the Hargrove estates so every room is ready for occupation if we need it. Don't fret over things, it's too early for that anyway. Wait to hear back, and then we'll work out the logistics."

"Thank you, Stevens, for the hearty talk. I will wait to worry."

He chuckled. "That's not exactly what I said, my lady, but it is best to wait and plan and then worry if things start to fall apart."

Sarah took the list Stevens had quickly written out for general information saying he would get the addresses updated and ready for her perusal later. She wanted to personally invite each family along with the more formal invitation which she planned to write out herself. Her father always complimented her handwriting, and she felt competent to complete that task. Now some of the others seemed daunting, but nothing she wouldn't tackle to make the family reunion, as she was beginning to think of it, a success.

Henry leapt off his horse at the stable and practically ran to the house, entering through the steward's door as the quickest means into the building. He was brought up short when he saw the shiny auburn head so close to the blond one of his steward. His young, handsome, unmarried steward.

"Stevens, how nice to find you working so closely with my countess. I assume this is a working meeting?"

He knew he sounded authoritarian, but couldn't prevent the cold edge to his voice. His first wife had taken a lover even before they married. Why should he believe his second would wait any longer?

Her welcoming smile died on her face and a blush suffused her cheeks trailing under the high collar on her dress. At least she wasn't dressed as a woman seeking to fill her bed with a strong attractive man.

"My lord," she said without any warmth.

His steward stood straighter and moved silently away from Sarah, but bowed as he said, "My lord, we were making the final tally of beds available for your family and their servants. I believe we will have more than enough even if they all come along with several servants per family."

The house party, of course. He had forgotten all about it and now he had spoiled his homecoming by showing what a jealous swine he was. "I must admit I forgot. It is just that this bill was finally put through and we lost by several votes. Now we must begin all over to right a wrong. I don't know how long it will take this next time." He had removed his hat upon entering and found his hand roughing his hair in anxious movements.

Sarah, her color returning to normal, said in a brittle tone, "How disappointing for you, my lord. Perhaps a hot meal will put you in a better mood?"

He felt sheepish and swatted the dust from his breeches with his crop. "Yes, I'm sure that will put me to rights. Are the children still awake?"

A softer expression crossed her face. "Yes, they hope each night you will return so try to stay up as long as they can. Michael falls to sleep first while Mary hangs onto hope the longest."

"Then I'll take myself up there." He turned to his steward saying, "I will speak with you in the morning and have you catch me up on things."

That man nodded, and he noticed his countess's mouth firm in a frown, but she did not excuse herself to go with him. He would have some fences to mend there.

As he strode into the nursery, seeing Mary's happy face and gleeful cry of welcome made all his blue-devils disappear. He lifted her into his arms and accepted the kiss on his cheek and hug around his neck. How he hated to leave his children even for something as important as this vote.

"I see Michael couldn't stay awake as long as you. Has he been a good boy while I've been away?"

"Yes. No more crying in the night. Mama says it's because he's got his teeth now." Her little brows came down in concern. "Where did he get them from, Papa?"

"Hm-m-m, that is a very good question and one I hope your mama can explain because now it is time for little girls to be asleep." He put her down as Lucy stood to take Mary's hand.

"Come, Lady Mary, and wash your hands and face. It is time for bed now."

"Papa, will you be here when I get up or must you go to London again?"

"I plan on being here for a long time now, Sugarplum. Maybe we can visit the stable tomorrow and see the horses. Do you think you and Michael will enjoy that?"

"Oh, yes. No one else likes the stables. Lucy thinks they smell bad."

His glance moved to the now blushing nursemaid, but he merely said, "Not all people can appreciate the scent of a fine horse. But I'll take you tomorrow, and perhaps you can talk your mama into going with us, as well."

"That will make it even more fun. I'll ask her when she comes in for breakfast."

That knowledge stopped his leaving as he asked, "Your mama eats here with you at breakfast?"

"Every morning since you've been away. Then we play games if it's rainy or go for a walk if it's fine. Are you coming for breakfast, too?"

"No, Sugarplum, your papa likes a big breakfast which would strain the arms of even the strongest of footmen to carry up three flights of stairs. I will meet with you after your porridge." He wondered if his wife would choose to eat with him or continue visiting the children so early.

His daughter yawned while nodding and quietly followed Lucy into another room.

Bathed, dressed in his banyan, and with the remnants of a meal on the table behind him, he worriedly paced in front of the adjoining door to his wife's suite. His gaze caught his reflection which showed an angry man with his hair standing on end from running his fingers through it in indecision.

Damnation! When he had to ride away from this house five days ago, he thought his life could get no better. He had happy children, well other than for Michael's teething, and a very responsive wife to warm his bed. He had spent hours dreaming of what he would teach her once he returned home. Now he was back, and he had stepped in it as soon as he entered the house.

Why would he jump to such a conclusion? He knew Sarah wasn't anything like his first wife. Did not have the need of men's adulation. Did not seek out men who would flirt and more to stroke her need to feel in control. Did not have a deceitful bone in her body.

He knew she was in her room. In fact, had been in there for at least half an hour alone since he heard Aggie leave her. Did he dare go in and apologize? Would it be enough to have her forgive his angry greeting? For embarrassing her in front of his steward? What would be the outcome if he ignored what had happened and met her over breakfast in the morning as if nothing untoward had occurred?

No, Mary told him Sarah was eating breakfast up in the nursery. So, if he were to have a dressing down by his new wife it needed to be tonight, and it needed to be now. He strode to the door and turned the knob hoping she hadn't locked it from her side.

Sarah heard the latch turn and the door open to show her husband standing in his robe and slippers. Her heart leapt to her throat. She feared his little contretemps would keep him from her bed—and she certainly didn't want that after waiting almost a week for his return to it. The one-night taste of heaven, the pleasure he had given her hadn't been enough, not nearly enough.

Not that she was going to allow his ill behavior to go unnoticed. His attitude was both embarrassing and humiliating—to both Stevens and her. Neither of them deserved Henry's bad opinion or his jumping to conclusions which had no basis in fact. It wasn't as if she and Stevens were in one another's arms, after all. They were finalizing the room assignments if everyone was available to travel for the reunion.

She would wait for Henry to set the tone. Was there going to be a confrontation, a denial, or an apology? She would gauge her reaction to his.

"I was tired, grumpy, and disappointed in the vote, but that is no excuse for verbally attacking you when I arrived home. I know you would never do or say anything that would show yourself in a bad light. My only excuse would be that I've felt dreadful since having to leave this house, leave you after what we shared the night before."

Sitting silently against the headboard and pillow for a moment she contemplated his punishment. Then decided by the appearance of his hair he had spent the past hour punishing himself and she wanted him in her arms, in her bed teaching her things she knew he knew. She pulled back the covers from the other side of the bed saying, "You must have had a dreadful time of it. We'll speak of it in the morning. For now, you need to rest."

She heard him exhale a long sigh as he left his slippers at the door and walked across the room to leave his banyan on the end of her bed. He was already aroused past a point of comfort, she was sure, as he climbed in next to her.

"You are a jewel among pearls, and I am so lucky to have you have the poor judgement of marrying me. I was surprised to find the door unlocked." He kissed her for a long moment before snuggling down onto the mattress with her in his arms.

"Don't be so smug. This isn't over, and I'm not sure I won't demand an apology to Stevens, also. He has been working late every night making sure the house party will be carried off in a manner befitting your family." She nestled into his neck and kissed the fur across his chest. He smelled of pine and lemon and had recently shaved. "Besides, you told me to beget a child consistent lovemaking was the best method, and I bow to your superior knowledge."

Covering her lips with his own for a few moments, he then whispered, "I'm glad you remembered some of my lesson. Now let's see how much of the rest you retained."

He proceeded to remind her of everything he had done the night before leaving her. Her body responded with enthusiasm. She realized she could touch him and he liked it, asking for more or firmer caresses, faster or slower strokes with which she obliged him. It pleased her to find ways to pleasure him. No matter what he thought, she was grateful for everything he gave her and for allowing her to mother his children, perhaps even father another onto her.

Their lovemaking was as fulfilling for them as the first night they spent together. She silently vowed to never allow little angers or hurt feelings come between them as man and wife.

Snuggling into his arms afterwards, she was feeling so at ease, so content. "I'm sorry your vote failed. Will they try again?"

She heard his sigh. "They will have to. Something must be done, and I wanted to be part of it, but after this trip…"

Patting his chest then leaving her hand there stroking him, she whispered, "You know we, the children and I, will return to town if it makes it easier for you. I know some of your bad temper was due to being away from them."

"From you. I was beside myself with fury for having to leave you just as we, well, you understand. I was afraid I would lose everything I'd gained in our relationship.

That I would lose you."

"Never. I made a vow, and mine are as strong as anyone's. Although I did not appreciate being thrown into the same category as your first wife, I understood seeing me alone with a man brought back bad memories."

"I never really thought you were up to anything and not only because I know Stevens is loyal to the bone. I know you, and I shouldn't have allowed myself leeway to take out my bad disposition on you. I cannot promise it won't happen again, but I think once I feel more confident in you, in your regard, the thought of you being unfaithful will never cross my mind."

She patted him knowing he wasn't over the pain and mistrust his first wife had instilled in him over so many years, no matter how much he declared Alicia's actions never hurt him. The woman left scars even if the actual wounds had healed. Sarah would remember how hurt, how betrayed she had felt when she realized the house on Curzon Street had never been meant for her whenever Henry showed signs of distrust. Eventually there would only be the two of them in this marriage, but it might be a while before that occurred.

CHAPTER NINE

"My lord," Sarah called out to Henry as he left the breakfast room. "Have you had time to mark the final family members and guests you wish to invite to the house party? I would like to finish the invitations and personal notes if you have done so."

He smiled and waited for her to catch up to him. How lovely she appeared in a rose-colored dress with lace at the sleeves and neckline. How young she looked for an old, tarnished man such as he. "I did as you requested this morning after hearing how important it was to get them sent out in time. I must say there wasn't much for me to do since Stevens has everything under control. He was correct in his assumption to invite all those who receive correspondence from me during the holidays. Best wishes for the new year and that sort of thing."

"Good, that means I'm almost done." She sounded breathless as she reached him, and he felt a tug deep inside as he remembered the other times her voice was low and breathless. He reached out to take her hand and held it.

"When are you going to return to eating breakfast with me, or must I resort to eating porridge with the children and you?"

She laughed and gazed up through her thick lashes. "We have poached eggs and toast soldiers some mornings."

"Add a pound of ham slices and kippers with that and I may be tempted."

"I'll bring the children down for the noon meal, and we will eat it in the breakfast dining room. Will that suit?"

"It's not simply seeing them which I intend to do once I've spoken and apologized to Stevens, but having you beside me."

She blushed and appeared so young and lovely he felt himself lean toward her for a kiss. She glanced around circumspectly for any servants then pursed her lips for a quick meeting of mouths. He wanted to continue with this dally, perhaps take her back upstairs, but then pulled himself away.

"I need to behave myself or find ourselves explaining more than we wish to the children or embarrassing the servants."

"I agree. The children and I will be down in an hour and ready for a walk then luncheon. Join us whenever you feel you can."

Another quick kiss on her lips and he allowed her to run away, moving quickly toward the stairs.

Watching the children chase a butterfly across the expanse of lawn, Sarah knew these halcyon days would soon be over. The leaves were already turning to fall colors, and all the butterflies and buzzing bees would be gone leaving only those birds hardy enough to survive an English winter.

Stroking her husband's back as he wore only his shirt sleeves was another luxury she allowed herself while sitting in the sunshine. He turned, bestowing one of his smiles on her, and her heart did a little flip. Would it always be like this or would they settle into a form of hibernation, too, as many of the other animals and insects did. Perhaps awaken in the spring for a few months of life?

"Henry, tell me about the cousins. I need to know something of them to be a good hostess. I wish to make sure there are enough entertainments available without overwhelming them. I want everyone time to catch up with family news, but not force everyone into merely sitting around drinking tea and listening to war stories."

"Well, with the younger ones you may have to take a guess. I was one of the older cousins, but some of the uncles aren't much older than I am. My mother's family was quite prolific, and she was the youngest, so when I came along there were a lot of us around the table as I remember… That didn't take into consideration the ones in the nursery."

"Who was the closest in age to you or the one you remember best?"

"Lucas. Lucas was the cousin I liked the best and probably the one most like me in temperament. He and I could always find something to amuse ourselves with and chose one another for any team event." He peered up to the sky evidently watching the clouds as they scurried across the sun causing a chill every once in a while.

"So, it was you and Lucas against the world?"

"Not really, although we both detested Timothy. Not sure why, but I think we knew, or at least we both felt, Timothy wasn't quite right. He liked to set traps for rabbits and then we found one mutilated one day. When we confronted Timothy with the evidence, he claimed another animal must have gotten to it. Lucas and I didn't believe him. Another animal would have eaten its fill then left. This poor creature had been tortured."

Sarah shivered and pulled the shawl closer around her neck.

He turned back to her. "Sorry, I forgot how gruesome that story was. I've never repeated what happened, and it's been decades ago."

"But I sent him an invitation. I wish I'd known." She didn't want that sort of memory raising its ugly head once the family was together again.

"I'm sure he's matured since then. He had an older brother who always ignored him and a mother who wouldn't stop coddling the older brother. Probably not the best combination for a boy who seemed jealous of what anyone else had. That's probably why Lucas and I stayed away from him. Timothy always seemed to want to get even with someone over imagined slights. I suppose he got over that, too, or he'd have been killed during a duel to assuage his honor by now."

Trying to lighten the mood, she added, "Now there is an activity for the men I didn't think of—dueling. Do you think I can find enough swords or pistols for this large of group?"

"No, but I suppose archery isn't out of the question."

"I have already thought about that if the weather holds. We have so many who are almost grown, but not quite out of the classroom. Several of the young women will be making their come-out next spring or fall."

"My God, how do you know that, woman? I couldn't even guess at most of their ages."

"Stevens gave me the return letters from your relatives this past year. Most send something in response to your holiday greeting which had bits of news like your uncle Byron's wife, Elise, is *enceinte* and are hoping for a boy since they have two girls already. Aunt Mildred had lumbago which pains her so in the cold weather." She saw his surprised expression. "You know the kinds of things family write to one another about."

"Yes, I know the kind of things since I read them as well. The thing is, I don't remember all that drivel. You are a font of information of my family members now, so there's another reason to keep you."

"You need more reasons?" She knew she had raised one eyebrow in disbelief.

"No, I have all the reasons I need." He pulled her forward toppling her onto his lap so he could lean over and kiss her lips as she giggled and wiggled in his arms.

"Oh, Papa, let my mama go." Sarah felt the weight of Mary land on Henry's back as he began to chuckle and gave her a final kiss before letting her loose.

He was red-faced and trying to peel Mary from his back and Michael from his arm without hurting either of them. "Now the dragon will have to eat one of you since you made him lose his captive queen. I suppose a princess is just as tasty." He grabbed Mary and made growling sounds against her tummy leaving her rolling on the ground chortling as he did the same with Michael who burst into giggles.

The sun hid behind the clouds again. Sarah hated to break up the idyllic day. "We all need to pack up our things and get inside. The sun seems to be gone for the day, and Michael will need to rest."

Mary moved slowly, dragging her feet. "Can you read about a dragon again, Mama? One who is friendly and becomes a pet."

"Certainly, but you must lie down and rest, too. If you fall asleep, I'll finish it tonight."

Sitting next to her husband in the breakfast room watching him put away a large pile of scrambled eggs as well as ham slices, Sarah tried to update him with the acceptances to the reunion. "I find it so rewarding that so many have responded already. I wanted to get the invitations out before they accepted other holiday house parties."

"I take it that pile of papers is from those accepting?"

"So far no one has sent their apologies although two of your aunts have specified needing separate beds for them and their spouses claiming snoring as the reason while two of your married cousins specifically asked to share a bed. Hm-m-m-m, probably an age thing. What do you think?"

"I think it depends on which aunt—some barely tolerate their husbands when they are awake. As for the married cousins, I agree wholeheartedly." He picked up her hand and placed a kiss on the palm.

"Stevens and I had figured the older couples would sleep separately already so there isn't a problem, and some have offered that their children can share. I suppose some do at home." She continued through the pile and then set them aside.

"I hope Cook and I have planned enough food." She gazed pointedly at his now empty plate as he finished his cup of coffee.

"By the amount on the bills I've received from the vendors, it seems as if we're planning to live out a siege by the French."

Stricken, she stared at him. "Am I spending too much? I can economize, but both you and Stevens said there was no need, and I wanted everything to be perfect for your family."

He grabbed her hand again and held it to his heart. "I was teasing, love. I don't even see the bills unless I ask for them and Stevens is correct, I can easily feed my family over the holidays."

"But I ordered extra hams and pork-bellies to be smoked, placed an order for cockles and eels from London, salted as well as fresh fish, venison and lamb from the home farm, three geese for Christmas dinner alone…"

Now he was laughing at her. "I'm sorry for laughing, I really am, but as you're naming off all these foods, I can only think how good they're all going to taste." He stood and kept hold of her hand. "I look forward to every meal, and so will the rest of my family. I wasn't aware that you had done so much of the minutiae."

"Well, yes, you must plan for these sorts of things. Cook and I put away extra preserves and made marmalade as well as dried extra herbs. You spoke of a siege, and I plan to feed an army. An army of various ages and palates, so I must serve something everyone will eat including the holiday fare like puddings and gingerbread everyone will expect."

"I demand you take a day of rest—with me. Leave the children in their nursery with Lucy and Mavis while you and I take a carriage out alone. It may be the last nice day for a while. It is what? A sennight before everyone arrives?"

"Most won't be here before the twentieth, which is still too soon for all the things I want to do."

"I want you to pay as much attention to me as you do these plans for my family. I hoped having you act as my hostess would bring us closer together." She knew his gaze searched her face, her eyes for an answer.

Setting all thoughts of the coming reunion aside, she nodded. She would like to spend time with him that wasn't merely to get her with child. The nights were still wonderful lying in his arms, but they never had any other time alone, not even immediately after their wedding. She began as a mother and then became a wife. Henry wanted a wife now, and she needed to please him as well as herself.

Dressed warmly to ward off the December chill, Henry drove them in a small open carriage she had never seen before. She put one arm through his and stuffed her gloved hand into the velvet muff the same color as the ribbon on her bonnet. She was glad the modiste, Madam LaFleur, had persevered and forced Sarah into procuring winter clothing as well as dresses for her immediate needs. Aggie was in raptures as each delivery unfolded more and more beautiful clothes. Not knowing what was expected of a countess, Sarah had to trust Madam's suggestions and found the woman's taste was moderate and very acceptable to Sarah. Henry didn't say anything about the bills or number of trunks for her personal clothes that had accompanied them to the country. He really was a very good husband.

Smiling up at him just as he glanced at her, she caught a wide smile cross his handsome face.

"What? Have I a smudge on my nose?" he teased.

"No, I was thinking of how blessed I am to have married a man such as you. So much out of my reach, my world, and then you offer me all that I ever wanted. Children, a lovely home, safety, and a means to satisfy my needs."

"Nothing about my title? I assure you it is old and distinguished." That grin was back on his face which seemed to show he was enjoying himself as much as she was.

"I'm not sure the title is an asset. Not that I disregard it, but you don't need a title to be the man I am grateful to have married. I feared I would not be up to being your countess. It all seemed so intimidating."

"Now anyone would think you were born to it. Look at the way the staff answer to you, go to you for instruction, the way you've taken on managing this reunion of strangers. It always felt too daunting for me or I would have held one long ago." He patted her hand and then took the reins in both hands again.

She knew she was blushing over his compliments and felt justified in her own pride of how far she had come since arriving in the country several weeks ago. It was like a different lifetime—like she was a different woman. But had she changed that much?

Running her father's home had entailed everything she had done this past two months only with less servants. Her father had a housekeeper with part time cleaning and washing maid, a footman and cook. Sarah had organized the meals and much of her father's personal correspondence and invitations. Since he had been a widower for years, most people forgot he had a grown daughter so she was not included. Besides, most were business contacts of her father's. Even the men who came to dinner with her father. Although she acted as his hostess, the conversations centered on business law and politics. This reunion was a culmination of everything she had learned in her father's home only on a larger magnitude.

"Cold?" he asked as he turned the horses onto a narrower path.

"No, very toasty." Then she peered around them. "I don't recognize this area at all. Are we still on Hargrove property?"

"Yes, this is the way to the oldest tenant I have. I thought I'd stop in to see how he fares. Stevens said he was feeling poorly with a cough last week. In someone that old it may be best if I send the doctor to him although I think it best if I talk him into it first or he may chase the poor man off with a pitchfork."

"Really? Is he a hermit then?"

Chuckling, Henry shook his head. "No, simply old and cranky and English. What else would you expect?"

"I expect to see a wizened, old man bent with age having a long white beard and hands gnarled with arthritis."

He gazed at her for a full minute before saying, "So you've met him already?"

Shaking her head and laughing she accepted his teasing. "That may have been a cliché, and I apologize." Staring toward the thatched roof and the chimney with a thin line of smoke rising into the air, she looked forward to this meeting. The old man must mean something to Henry if he took time out of his day for a visit as well as having Stevens check on him.

The door to the cottage opened as the horses came to a stop. A man appearing exactly as Sarah described him stood in the opening waving for them to enter. She glanced quickly at her husband who still maintained his grin.

"My lord, welcome. My lady, would you care for tea?"

Seeing as he had some already brewed and not wanting him to think she wouldn't accept his hospitality, she nodded. "It is a little nippier than I thought when we set out for our ride." She removed her gloves and sat at the table near the teapot.

Henry removed his top hat and gloves setting them on the corner of the table before sitting down as well.

"Bread and butter, my lord?" The man brought a half loaf over with a covered dish of what she thought held butter.

Her husband raised his hand in denial. "Oh, no, we ate a hearty meal before leaving, and I dare not eat another thing, but go ahead if we have interrupted your meal."

"I remember when any offer of food was accepted. Of course, you were a growing boy back then so that makes sense." He turned toward Sarah with what she thought was a smile since the beard was not only white but fluffy and hid most of his features. "My lady, it is good to meet you. My niece tells me she is right glad to have you at Hargrove. Makes it seem like a home again."

Now Sarah was confused. "Your niece?"

Henry explained, "Mrs. Cushions. She's home grown as some call it. Many of my staff originated here on the estate, and a better bunch of people would be hard to find."

She knew he was saying that to compliment the old man and his family. "I was so lost taking over such a large establishment. I can't say enough about how much help Mrs. Cushions has been. I'm not sure we could have held this family gathering without her."

The man nodded as he poured her a cup and then one for Henry and finally one for himself ignoring the bread and butter, but offering her sugar and milk. "She's been that excited each time I see her. Comes and brings me fresh bread and things. A sweet girl, she is."

Realizing he was talking of her middle-aged housekeeper Sarah took a sip of the tea. "This is very good."

"Should be, my lady, it comes from your own pantry." The man spoke unapologetically as he took a long drink then wiped his beard.

A cough caught her unaware and, as she choked, met the crinkled eyes of her husband who blandly took a drink of his tea. She was wiping tears forming in her eyes with her fingers when Henry finally spoke up and took the attention off of her.

"Samuel, Stevens said you had a cough. Is it gone already?"

"Yes, my lord, it was a bit of ague from working in the early morning dew. I told Stevens I'd be right as rain in a few days, but the boy worries. Guess he doesn't want to be responsible for me dying on his watch. But realistically, it's going to happen at some point."

"That's the way of life." Henry seemed to be thinking of other lives ended, but she couldn't tell if it was his first wife or past people like his father. "The option to growing older isn't very appealing to most of us though."

The old man raised his cup. "Right you are, my lord, so we all simply keep going until the good Lord calls us home."

Henry stood and put out his hand to shake the old man's before turning to her. "My lady, are you ready to brave the cold air once more?"

"Of course, my lord. Thank you for the hospitality

and tea, Mr., er, Samuel."

The man followed them to the door and waited for them to drive off before closing the cold out and the heat from his fire in. She sat back and marveled at the man and his opinion of life. "He's quite a character, isn't he?"

"I've always thought so. When you described him, I thought for sure you had met or Mrs. Cushions had said something. The woman visits often when we are in the country. I think she is the only relative he has although everyone takes care of him when she's in town with the household."

"I never considered how an estate like this is like a town in itself. It produces most of what it needs, families live and die within its borders, look toward the landowners for most of their welfare. Was Mrs. Cushions' mother the housekeeper before her?"

"No, she was my mother's lady's maid and trained for the position from the time she was twelve. I guess everyone I employ, except Stevens, began their career here. In a way, he did as well since his father was steward to my father and, when he retired, the son took over. Quietly and without fanfare. There was hardly a nod to the older man leaving although he received a severance package, I know. There are several retainers living on the estate as well."

Excited by this news, she asked, "Who? Is your old governess here?"

"No, Maudie passed away while I was in school. I was sent away when I was nine, and she was elderly for all the years that I can remember."

"You sound like you liked her." She found she wanted to know what he was like as a child to help her gauge what Michael will be like or any child she had.

The thought of his child growing in her brought a flush of warmth through her entire body.

"I had a happy childhood, Sarah. I loved my father and although we didn't spend much time together due to his schedule and my schooling there wasn't any contention between us. My mother died in childbirth when I was still a toddler. Maudie was the only mother I remember and, of course, all the cousins. I know there were aunts and uncles as well, but it was the children I ran with during the summers when their parents tried to find relief from the town's heat and odors."

"And we are back to why I'm planning a house party for forty or so, plus servants."

"Exactly, and I am looking forward to seeing the cousins more than I thought possible. I have only seen Lucas and met his wife, Eleanor, in town, but I never accepted any of their invitations for dinner since by then Alicia and I had come to an agreement. We spent our lives living separately."

"Then I am glad they were the first to write with their acceptance. They have three children, you know, so that means Mary and Michael will have cousins to play with also."

"That was part of the plan, wasn't it? To give our children family to hold on to no matter what may happen to us?" He glanced down to see her reaction.

"Yes, of course, for the children." Then leaned her head against his arm. "Henry, would you mind if we returned home now? I want us to have time with them before their dinner."

"I think that is a good idea. We can have our alone time later in your room."

Burying her face into his sleeve, she nodded,

remaining quite as she thought of what that alone time would incorporate.

CHAPTER TEN

Sarah was nervous as she watched the line of carriages come up the drive. Bates stood at attention as if this was an ordinary occurrence while a line of maids formed to the side out of the way ready to lead guests to their rooms and make sure everything was to their liking. This included the tweenies and anyone else presentable enough to do so. Everyone wore new uniforms and caps as required, white gloves repaired or replaced, and starched aprons as expected. Her staff could have passed a king's inspection, and watching them renewed her own confidence. She felt secure in knowing nothing had been left undone or slipshod

Henry stepped out to the stone drive even though the December weather had finally arrived. No snow which Sarah wouldn't have been displeased with, but there had been frost in the morning and a sudden lack of birds flitting from tree to tree.

He greeted the people as they climbed down from the large travelling coach. "Lucas. Eleanor. I was hoping you would be one of the first. I admit to not knowing many of the younger cousins and am looking for some guidance from both of you."

Henry shook hands with the tall man, dark like Henry, and the woman, who Sarah knew to be his wife. This was the cousin Henry most wished to see, to connect with after all these years, and it seemed as if it were the same for Lucas. His eyes remained on Henry as he introduced three young children who would be the perfect ages to play with Mary and Michael in the nursery. A nurse stepped down from the carriage and stood trying to corral the little ones who had an overabundance of energy after riding for hours.

She hated to disrupt the reacquaintance, but there were other carriages arriving as well as it being chilly standing in the open as they were. "Henry, allow them to step inside at least, dear. Lucy is here to take the children upstairs to the nursery where they can warm up and have something to eat if they wish."

The nursemaid practically sagged with relief and then gathered the hands of two of the children with the third trailing behind obligingly. The adults laughed to find themselves standing outside in the cold, and Lucas escorted his wife toward Sarah.

"You must be Cousin Sarah." He pulled her into his arms and placed a kiss on her cheek and then turned her to his wife who did the same. "I was so glad to receive your letter, I made sure to clear our calendar so we could stay the entire time. I loved coming here in my youth."

Sarah liked them both immediately. Henry said this man was his favorite cousin, and she could see why. Nothing fake about him at all, and his wife seemed as open as Lucas.

"We will make ourselves scarce, Cousin Sarah, so you can welcome the others. We have already run into most of this group at the inns along the way so will miss nothing. I assume you want us in one of the parlors?" Eleanor asked as she watched her brood herded toward the doorway.

"Yes, one of the footmen can show you the way to

the blue parlor or to your rooms whichever you prefer."

"If there's tea planned in the parlor then that's where I'd like to be," Eleanor said gratefully.

Sarah replied, "Yes, everything should be ready. I'll come as soon as these carriages are seen to."

That may have been an optimistic promise since the stream of conveyances never seemed to stop coming. A quick greeting and introduction were all she could hope for as everyone was tired of riding at this point. Many had been on the road for a couple of days. Long enough to be bored with constant bouncing and swaying although most did not complain other than to say they were glad to have arrived.

She and Henry remained outside as yet another carriage arrived. Sarah's enthusiasm hadn't diminished in the least. "This is exciting now I've met a few of your relatives, Henry. They all seem so pleased to be back here and seeing one another."

He merely smiled and waited to see who would emerge from the newly stopped carriage. The footman lowered the step and opened the door—for the most gorgeous woman Sarah had ever seen. Familiar features held in a precise manner had Sarah grabbing her husband's arm for support. It was exactly like the drawings in the Curzon house. The same as the large portrait that had been hanging in the master suite when she had arrived at the London town house. Before it had been removed and taken to the attic until one of the children wanted it for their home.

Henry's expression froze in displeasure which helped calm Sarah. Evidently this woman, who resembled his dead wife, did not bring with her any fond memories. The opposite perhaps.

"Sarah, I introduce Lady Cavanaugh, Alicia's sister." Turning to the smiling woman with the superior expression on her face, he continued, "I didn't know you had received an invitation, Althea."

"Well, in truth, I came to spend this first holiday without their mother with my favorite niece and nephew. I know how difficult holidays can be without close relatives. But I see you've risen above your grief and are throwing a party. How brave of you—both." The woman's cold gaze moved between Sarah and Henry as if calculating each of their responses.

Henry spoke in their defense. "I have resurrected the gathering my family always held this time of year. I plan on continuing with all of them when summer rolls around."

"I'm glad to see my sister's death hasn't hampered your enthusiasm for life." The other woman gave a cold glance toward Sarah, but otherwise seemed to have dismissed her from the conversation. This had become a battle between Henry and Lady Cavanaugh.

Sarah decided she needed to step in before this turned ugly. "There are empty beds in the single ladies' chamber. I'm sure there is a maid inside waiting to take you up." She noted the numerous trunks still on the conveyance and the lady's maid waiting for directions. The footmen began removing the trunks at her nod.

Another large carriage pulled into sight, and Lady Cavanaugh glided toward the door as if she owned the place. This wasn't anyone she and Henry had discussed. Seeing the woman who resembled Henry's first wife so closely had unsettled Sarah once again. Now trepidation filled her as she faced an unknown visitor.

Henry's family was punctual, at least, and soon

everyone was happily settled in by the late supper. Sarah noted a coolness between Lady Cavanaugh and almost all the others. No love lost there, at least, so Sarah needn't fear a conspiracy. Perhaps the woman's untimely visit was exactly as she said. A time to be with her sister's children during this holiday season. At least there will be plenty of others to keep Sarah busy so she didn't focus on the one woman who might be able to bring everything crashing down upon them.

Snuggling down in her husband's arms that night, she exhaled a long sigh.

Henry pulled her closer. "Was it that arduous? I thought it went quiet well."

"For our first time hosting such an event, I must admit we had less problems than I thought although it is early days yet." She pushed his immovable chest to emphasize her next comment. "And you could have told me that your Aunt Gertrude and your grandmother did not get along. I wouldn't have put them in one of the suites as I had. Now I'm worried one or the other will ask to be moved, and we don't have another suitable room. The one left without a private parlor will feel abused, I'm sure."

"I honestly forgot they had quarreled. I don't think they even remember why they don't like one another. Give them a chance to get reacquainted before moving either of them. Don't worry about everyone so much."

"Did you know your great aunt brings her own special tea with her? It's the only thing she drinks, but at least her lady's maid makes it for her. Seems she's the only one to steep it properly to Great Aunt Gertrude's taste."

"She would have made do I'm sure with what you

had available. My last trip to the basement I thought I was in a shop the shelves were so full." He nudged her as he spoke.

"But I want them to be happy. I want them to remember this place like you do." She relayed her deepest fear. "I want them to think you didn't marry beneath your rank. That you married a woman worthy of you and of being your countess."

"Need I make love to you again to show you what I think of anyone else's opinion? I married a woman I thought would make a wonderful mother to my children, a woman who was honest and true to her word, a woman well worth being my countess. If anything, seeing my family here this evening around the dining table ensured me I had done the right thing. No one is going to convince me there is a better woman out there in the world for me."

Sarah broached what neither of them had mentioned. "Do you think Lady Cavanaugh knows. I mean, would she be the kind to blurt out intimate facts about her sister and, um, would she try to ruin this for us?"

He sighed and placed his arm behind his head. "I never found her to be much different from her sister, I'm afraid. As the eldest, she expected to marry first, and I had thought of her as a possibility for my countess in the beginning. Somehow, Alicia was always the one there when I arrived for a visit. Even asked for my name to be placed on her dance card which I must admit I found gratifying. She seemed to enjoy being with me and not because I held a title." He scoffed. "Of course, it was all due to the limited time she had to snare a husband before things became obvious as to her condition. I had actually felt quite smug about the whole thing. She was a good actress, and I fear her sister has the same ability. I hope she gets bored with the children and leaves soon."

"You think that is best?"

"I know Mary doesn't care for her, and this will be the first time Althea has seen Michael. I can only think she's here for some other reason than for a holiday visit. She and Alicia were barely more than civil to each other, and the number of times those sisters even spoke to one another after the marriage can be counted on one hand." He rolled to his side and pulled her closer. "We shall not waste any more time thinking about her. I'm sure she will get bored and leave once her curiosity about my sudden marriage and then holding this house party so soon fades. You and I have more important things to do."

"You, say the sweetest things, Henry, that sometimes I almost believe you." She felt the kiss on the top of her head as she dozed off.

The men had all disappeared to various rooms to play cards or billiards or make themselves scarce while the women gathered to gossip and catch up with family news in the large blue parlor. It was one of the rooms large enough to seat so many at one time. Sarah was stepping in when a voice rose above the others.

"Is that my great nephew's wife, Sarah? Let me see you, gel. Come closer to the window light."

Sarah's heart dropped for she already knew that voice. It was that of the most prestigiously titled personage there. The Duchess, or better known as Great Aunt Gertrude to those in the family. Sarah turned immediately, took a few steps, and made her curtsy. "Your grace?"

"Just as I thought. It came to me last night where I

had seen you before…"

Panic caused sweat to dampen her camisole as she faced the intimidating woman. The conversations had all ceased as eyes watched the drama unfolding in front of them. This woman had a reputation of tearing others to shreds if they did not please her and, although Sarah had done nothing to displease the woman, she had put her in the same suite with the only other relative of a similar age. A woman Sarah had later learned did not get along with the duchess. Sarah remained standing trying not to let her knees knock loudly enough for others to hear.

The duchess continued and nodded. "Yes, you have the look about you. Tell me, was your grandmother by any chance Lady Caroline Carlton?"

Relief rushed through her. "Why, yes, your grace, although I was quite small when she passed. My father spoke of her often, and I have seen a miniature of her holding my father in her arms."

"I knew her before that. We came-out the same year. She married her viscount and I married my duke. We lost touch except for the yearly letters to one another. Court duties took up much of my life, and I was no longer my own master. But that year…we had so much fun together. She was a breath of fresh air. When we attended the same balls or parties I was ensured of many good times. Seeing you brings back those memories so keenly. You are so like her in many ways."

"Thank you, your grace, although I never knew her. My father was quite fond of her and had said I resembled her physically."

The woman leaned forward on her cane as she sat on the sofa. "I think you resemble her more than merely physically. She had a sense of right that I envied. My parents were very controlling, but they allowed me to befriend Caro. She knew what to say to put anyone in their place and left them wondering if they had been outmaneuvered. Of course, they had, but by then she and I would be off to another group."

"She sounds as if we would have gotten along very well. Growing up without a mother has made me rather independent, I'm afraid."

"Oh, no, don't apologize, my dear. Women need to speak up for themselves more often. We should seek the vote as men did and help run this country. Queens did it, so why shouldn't women everywhere have the same opportunity?"

Sarah smiled at the older woman now on a tirade. "I agree since I bow to your experience and knowledge which is so much greater than mine."

The Duchess chuckled. "Exactly what Caro would have said. I like you, Sarah, and I like what I see is happening here this season. We will need to find time to have tea in my parlor where I can tell you more about your grandmother."

Sarah curtsied again. "I look forward to those times."

The other conversations started up again, and Sarah felt a rush of relief. Several of the other women nodded toward her, and their smiles seemed more real. Evidently the women of the family had been waiting for some sign as to how they were supposed to accept Henry's new wife. The acceptance by the duchess had sealed Sarah's welcome into his family.

Eleanor was telling Sarah which agency she had hired the governess for her daughter from when the butler came in and whispered that there was another carriage arriving. Sarah excused herself peering around the convivial room noting those present seemed occupied talking to one another. Since everyone who had sent back an acceptance was already there, she followed Bates out of the room to greet this new arrival. Perhaps it was a local who was unaware of the large family gathering already taking place. She sent a footman to find her husband in case it was a neighbor and she needed his introduction to them.

She stood outside. The air was nippy, but not unduly so considering it was almost Christmas. Once the carriage stopped there seemed to be several moments of quiet as the footman stood near the door waiting for permission to open it. Finally, a voice from inside indicated they were ready to disembark. A lone occupant stepped down, appearing bored as he gazed around ignoring Sarah as she waited to greet him—whoever he was.

Finally, his lazy eyes landed on her, and a smile crossed his face. He was a handsome man, but not attractive which Sarah thought odd since she had always thought the two went together as with her husband. This man was haughty, the smile a means to get his way and appeared as if he never cared for everyone besides himself. Sarah felt he thought highly of himself. His face also seemed to lack the robustness of her husband's seeming to lean toward a grey paleness.

His clothes, although the height of fashion, were in dishabille as if his valet hadn't tended to him before he had left for his journey. The lace of his cravat wasn't starched nor possibly even ironed. A button on his cuff hung by a thread indicating again a lack of care.

Thankfully she heard Henry behind her. "Timothy,

we weren't expecting you since you never made the effort to respond to the invitation."

Her husband, usually so accommodating, sounded angry as if their pleasant family reunion had been invaded by vipers—or at least one.

"Cousin, I had planned on staying in London at a house party, but things changed last minute." In a sotto voice added as if all those present couldn't hear him, "The lady's husband returned from the country, and I needed to make a hasty escape. I arrive as you see me, less my servant and valise. I will need some change of clothes and, since we are of a similar size, I will have to don your less than fashionable wardrobe." The story sounded plausible, but for some reason Sarah thought he dissembled.

Placing a quizzing glass in one eye, he walked directly toward Sarah who was now shivering from standing and waiting so long. "Now who is this lovely creature? Cuz, have you been holding out on me?"

Henry stepped between the two of them. "If you had but read your invitation instead of tossing it into the fireplace as I assume you had, you would realize this gathering was partly to introduce my wife to the family."

Timothy loomed over her. His breath reeked of strong liquor making her blink back tears. "Wife, hmmm? That is a pity, but I'm sure there may be others."

"Only you, Timothy, would attend a family reunion in search of a willing woman." Henry sounded disgusted with this cousin, which did not surprise Sarah. Only that her husband hadn't piled this man into his carriage and sent him back to London did. "Let us get inside. My wife, Lady Hargrove, is freezing." She thought that was going to be as much of an introduction as the man was going to get and was glad of it. Thinking that this man might hold her hand or kiss the back of it made her stomach lurch, the sensation taking her by surprise.

Even with the addition of Timothy, the dining table was a festive event again that evening. No one other than the two eldest ladies seemed to welcome Timothy with any warmth, and he didn't try to ingratiate himself with anyone besides the eldest of the family. Eleanor said it was because his pockets were to let and he was hoping when the older ladies 'kicked the bucket' he'd be remembered in their wills. Both of the elderly female relatives, Great Aunt Gertrude and Grandmother, had money to award as they wished once they were gone.

Sarah appreciated Eleanor's friendship and her knowledge of the family noting that most of the other women gravitated to her as well. That evening they were planning a musical night with various children followed by a few of the wives entertaining the others on the pianoforte, harp, and other instruments already in the music room. Plenty of sitting places were brought in, and that is where the serving of the after-dinner tea occurred.

Impressed with the amount of talent the family had, Sarah thought she might add a few other nights of similar activities. She also noted Timothy spent his evening at the back of the room drinking. Pouring his own glassfuls from the decanter he had found somewhere in the house. At least it kept him occupied, and he hadn't said anything inappropriate while the younger family members were in the room.

That soon ended and, as his voice rose, most of the ladies decided to leave for their bedchambers. The two elderly women, the women Timothy needed to impress, had already left. Eleanor whispered as she left the room,

"If Tim thinks his behavior will go unnoticed by his grandmother, he is very mistaken. That woman has eyes in the back of her head, I swear."

When the last of the ladies headed to their beds, Sarah waved to Henry who was still conversing with Lucas, and his slight nod let her know he would be up to their room shortly as well.

CHAPTER ELEVEN

Sarah ran into Henry and the other men gathering in the foyer. She gazed approvingly at the older boys who had been included in the hunting and cutting of greenery for the wreaths and decorations. All were bundled up as if planning for a snow storm. Although the weather was a little misty, Henry didn't think there would be more than the present light snow anytime soon.

Making sure Henry's scarf was secure, she stood in front of him. "The footmen will go with you to do the actual cutting. Thank you for taking the boys. It's so difficult finding something to entertain them."

"Entertain them? No, I'm taking them because I'm not shimmying up trees to cut mistletoe or collect holly berries." He smiled so she knew he was teasing her.

"Thank you, anyway. I knew I could count on you," she said patting his coat closed.

She leaned toward him, but he resisted the urge to kiss her goodbye. After all, none of the other wives were here to do so and they were only going to the Homewood not off to battle. As soon as she stepped away, he was sorry he hadn't taken advantage of the offer and to hell with the rest.

Henry strode behind the others taking advantage of watching the family members along with two footmen trudging ahead. They were like an army on the march with a couple of the younger men almost running and

145

pointing at anything still green in the light dusting of snow. A shout of: "There some is," rang out. Several men ran to watch Hugo climb a tree and pull down a clump of mistletoe.

"Well done! Now on to the holly!" Henry called out cheerfully as they all began running ahead.

Lucas came closer chuckling at the enthusiasm. "Were we ever that young and undignified?"

"I remember climbing an apple tree to impress Sally Wright one summer."

Nodding, Lucas finished, "Then falling out of it with the wrong apple in your hand. I had to retrieve the correct one before she bestowed a smile on either of us. What ever happened to her?"

"She's Lady Withers now and has who knows how many children." They marched on barely keeping the group in sight.

Lucas stopped and gaped at him. "How do you keep track of everyone?"

Shrugging, Henry admitted, "I have a very good steward who keeps me updated with anyone I have sent letters to. He acts as my informal secretary, as well."

"I leave all that up to Eleanor who does a good job keeping me informed of births and deaths. I go to the weddings she tells me are important, and I tell her when I wish time off to go to the races or horse auctions. A perfect marriage." Lucas smiled to let his cousin know he was teasing and that his wife meant much more to him than anything else.

Henry trudged on now hearing the sound of an ax cutting through solid wood. "Must have found the yule log the gamekeeper marked a few weeks back although he said it was too long for any of the fireplaces except the one in the ballroom."

Lucas raised his eyebrows in surprise. "Going all out for this holiday season, aren't you, old man? Do I have it right that this is due to your new wife?"

"Yes, I guess I can lay it at her door although she made it a holiday thing. We were discussing family members, and I began to reminisce about such gatherings, and it blossomed from there."

"I guess I can tell you that Eleanor and I both like Sarah. She is exactly the kind of wife you should have always had."

Henry pursed his lips. "I wish you would tell her that. She's a little hesitant with things since she doesn't feel she is worthy to be my countess."

Turning he felt Lucas' gaze on him. "Why in the world not?"

Henry wasn't sure he wanted to tell his cousin the reason behind Sarah's feelings of inferiority, but thought he needed to share to make sure no one else thought the same way his wife did. "She wasn't a lady. She's the great granddaughter of a viscount, but descendent of a second son from a second son. You know how it goes. She doesn't feel she can be a proper countess without that ton-ish blue-blood. A lot of good it did Alicia."

"I must agree with that sentiment even though you didn't ask. How did you two meet if she isn't used to being in society?"

A deep breath, and Henry debated again. Exhaling, he finally admitted to everything. "I'm sure you know Alicia was with child when I married her." He allowed Lucas to merely nod as they picked their way over the uneven ground before continuing. "I was not the father." Lucas's head snapped up.

"I knew Mary wasn't mine although not until after she was born, and by then I was in love with the little mite. It wasn't her fault I was tricked into marriage." He allowed himself a smile as he thought of how tiny Mary was and how perfect from her dark curls to her large bright eyes. "I thought there was still hope for my marriage, and Alicia promised never to stray again. I accepted her word but watched her closely. Finally, she agreed to give me an heir if I would allow her freedom once she bore a boy. As you know, the next child she had was a son, and there is no doubt he is mine, so I gave her what she wanted."

Lucas stopped and put his hand out as if to give comfort. "I'm so sorry, Henry. I wish there had been some way I could have helped. I realized you were always alone when we ran into one another, but I hadn't realized it was that way all the time for you. Did you at least have mistresses for comfort?"

"No, my vows kept coming to the forefront. I'm an adult and came to an adult decision. If Alicia didn't want to remain faithful to her vows, I was not going to become a jailer to force her to do so. She wanted to paint, and I agreed to pay for an art master and ignore the fact she no longer slept at home every night."

Aghast, Lucas asked, "She was having a liaison with an artist?"

"No, actually she had gone back to the man who fathered Mary. She went back to Sarah's husband."

Lucas took a moment to understand the convoluted relationships. "You're telling me Sarah was married to the man Alicia was sleeping with? How did you...how did she...do I even want to know?"

"It gets better. If any of this ever got out the gossip

papers would have a heyday with it." Lucas waved away the thought of ever telling anyone. "As I wrote to everyone, Alicia was killed when the carriage she was riding in rolled over. Sarah's husband had been the driver, and they were returning from a tryst at a country inn."

"So, Sarah knew of the affair?"

"No, not until she found their love nest over on Curzon Street and I ran into her there. We have neatened up the story of how we met, but that is the truth of the matter. Sarah doesn't like the dissembling of it all and tries not to tell anyone anything." He peered around realizing they had lost sight of the group although he could hear voices in the distance.

"I understand. Eleanor would probably feel the same way, but you were both the innocent parties in all this. No one should hold these events against either of you."

"I agree although if the truth got out then Mary would be deeply affected no matter how much I told her she was my daughter, had always been my daughter."

"And to all intents and purpose she is. It is amazing you and Sarah found one another and realized what was between the two of you." Lucas began walking toward the voices.

"What do you mean? Sarah and I decided it would be best for the children. Mary in particular to have family close to her. Sarah never had children, but wanted a family so I proposed. So far, I have no complaints."

Lucas stopped Henry and stared him in the face. "Do you really think that what you and Sarah have is common? Eleanor and I were speaking of it this morning as we dressed. Of how good you two are together, of how caring you are of the children, of how you share so much with one another throughout the day. We've never seen another couple, besides ourselves, so close. There must be more to this than she wanted children and you needed a mother for yours…"

Henry shook his head and started forward once again. "No, no more than that."

Lucas accepted that the confidence was over and ran toward the tree Terrance was beginning to climb to give the boy a boost up. Henry watched, going over the past conversation wondering if he had missed something Lucas and Eleanor seemed to think was there.

It was easy to feel married, truly married, to Sarah even before they had shared a bed. The closeness was there as soon as he had seen her with his children. He could see them as a loving family from the first, and she seemed to feel the same. It was different than with Alicia, but he had expected it would be.

Alicia was the daughter of a viscount and had been raised to expect certain things from life. One of those things was a titled husband with money, and Henry admitted he knew there had been other men in the running. When Alicia had allowed him more leniency with her body, he thought he had been singled out as being the one—the man who won her heart. The need for an expedient wedding was an unfortunate outcome, but not something he worried over. They were certainly not the only couple with a seven-month wonder in the ton.

After Mary's birth and Alicia's refusing his advances, he put it down as a young girl's fear of going through childbirth again—even after he realized he wasn't Mary's father. Still, he held on to the idea the marriage vows would assure their family consistency.

How naïve of him. Thinking that giving her an

unlimited clothing budget, bringing home gifts of jewelry and trinkets, paying attention to her and asking to escort her to entertainments would ensure her willingness to be his wife again. But a year went by and her cold shoulder was all he had received—that and complaints of boredom, yearning to go places without him, and discontent at being his wife.

Then their contract—if she provided an heir, he would grant her the freedom she required as long as she was discreet. That was the one issue he had insisted upon. Not for himself, but for the children. He never wanted anyone to discover Mary's paternity or for Michael to think any less of his mother when he grew to adulthood. Henry promised himself he would keep her secrets as long as she lived. He still limited the information and regretted having told Lucas although he trusted his cousin not to pass it on to anyone besides Eleanor. Henry understood now the bond between some married couples and at how close they were. Truly one body and mind.

The urge to return to the house and seek out his wife was strong. How pathetic he would seem even to Lucas if he had done that. Shaking his head at the sad state of affairs, he hurried to help gather the holly onto the canvas to be dragged back. A smile spread across his face as he thought of the delight Sarah would have over all this bounty.

Sarah watched as the men and boys trudged out noisily with two burly footmen following behind and hurried to make sure everyone had something to do and felt included in the holiday festivities. The ladies as well as some of the older girls not yet out of the schoolroom were sitting in the blue parlor doing various needlework projects. It had been difficult for Sarah to think of some way to make this younger age group feel a part of the festivities. Although they were at the evening table for meals, they fell between what the nursemaids planned for the little ones and what adults found entertaining. Sarah had planned on everyone having fun while getting to know the rest of the family at the same time.

"Melissa and Bethany, would you like to add sparkles to these? First you must cut out the flower shapes from the cloth, paint them with this glue and sprinkle the tiny crystals onto them and set them to dry. I want to add them to the wreaths we'll make once we get the greenery." Sarah was rewarded by both girls jumping up from the footstools they had been sitting on and studied the project set out for them.

"These should look lovely nestled in greenery, Cousin Sarah," Bethany said as she picked up one of the many pairs of scissors set out. It had been decided the first day since they were all family with many titled ladies and gentlemen, those honorifics would not be used. Besides, Sarah was not used to being referred to as 'my lady' even though all the staff had been using the term since her marriage.

"Sarah, come tell me if this is right. The angel's wings seem off to me." Henry's grandmother held up the white crocheted angel for all to observe. Work stopped as the women examined it closely.

Sarah explained as everyone nodded and went back to their own work. "That's lovely. It only needs one more row and then you can finish the edges. I'll dip it in starch and let it dry overnight so it will be ready to use tomorrow also."

"I'm a little unused to doing handwork that calls for

this fine of stitching, but Gert lent me her spectacles and everything is so much clearer." The older woman gave faint praise to her sister-in-law.

Great Aunt Gertrude interrupted, "I've been telling you for ages that you were blind as a bat. I can see well enough without them to knit. Anyone can knit even in the dark."

"Gert, I agree my eyesight might be a tad bit less than what it was. I'll see to getting fitted for a pair of spectacles as soon as we get home." Then they both returned to their work.

Sarah observed the work glad that everyone so far seemed content with their projects. She would have the loveliest wreaths in the county. "I'll go and see how the others are doing." There were a few murmurs of acknowledgement, but everyone continued with their craft.

Following the high-pitched voices, Sarah found the children covered in powdered sugar and marzipan. "Um-m-m-m, you all smell and look so delicious. I could eat you up." She nuzzled Michael who was standing on a chair next to his nursemaid and heard him giggle with glee.

Mavis gave a guilty smile. "We thought with all of us, we could keep the untidiness down to a minimum, but with so many little hands all wanting to make a gingerbread man it seems we have a bit of a mess." The other nursemaids watched Sarah with wide frightened eyes.

"That's what holidays are for, aren't they? They start out a little messy, but it all gets cleaned up in the end. Besides, the children seem to be having a great time, and those are tasty looking gingerbread men even if some are missing their eyes."

Mary, pointing out a dough-man appearing a little worse for wear said, "Mine has two eyes, Mama. And I tried to help Michael, but he keeps eating his raisins off."

Sarah grabbed one of the unclaimed raisins sitting on the table and popped it into her mouth. "Hm-m-m-m," her head nodding, "eyes taste good."

The children laughed, and she waved as she left them to their fun. She didn't envy the nursemaids bathing those children tonight. Getting dough out of little ones' curls was going to be a chore.

Calm at last. Sarah closed the door on the conservatory and leaned back against the windowed door. Peace and quiet, who would have thought how good that felt with a houseful of family. Everyone was getting along well, even the staff was working in tandem and she really couldn't have wished for a more congenial group. All except Timothy, of course, who yesterday complained about everything from the meal offerings to the quality of brandy although it didn't stop him from emptying another decanter.

Picking up the shears, she went to the flowering plants kept ready for this event. These too had to be treated special so that the blooms were fresh and ready to use for the centerpieces on the dinner table. It must seem as if that is all that's going on to the kitchen staff. Breakfast drags out as everyone rises when they wish and then luncheon, afternoon tea, and the large dinner each evening. That doesn't account for the staff's or children's meals. She would need to get Cook and Mrs. Cushions nice gifts for all the extra work this reunion had caused.

Tonight's table would have fall colors since she

wanted to leave the red blooms for Christmas Eve and Day. The copper-colored mums were first followed by golden black-eyed Susan. She jumped when a voice too close interrupted her pleasant thoughts.

"Well, look what we have here just when I thought I would be bored to death."

To say she was startled by the man was not strong enough. She tried not to let it show in her voice. "Timothy. What an odd place to find you. I would have thought you with the other men."

"What, and get pitch on my fine clothes? Not a chance. I only ride when I need to. Otherwise, I spend my time inside—a house, a carriage, a woman." He let the last word stretch out, but Sarah wasn't going to show her disquiet at the comment. She'd been widowed and re-married, and his words weren't going to cause her discomfort. She decided to ignore him thinking that speaking would set his interest in trying to unsettle her composure.

"Come now, don't pretend you're not used to dalliance outside the bounds of matrimony? After all, my dear cousin's wife, Alicia, wasn't very firm with her vows. I saw her with a lover at a gaming hell one evening in London. Not many women there so she stood out. Can't say I saw much of her, of course. She begged me not to tell, but then who was I to tell anyone who would care? Henry had stopped speaking to me years before. Besides, I didn't owe him anything. Let him take care of his own wife. I wasn't her keeper."

"But you didn't get the man's name?" She didn't think Timothy knew her married name, but he could learn it from a past London Times. All marriages of titled persons were printed.

"No, didn't matter to me. No one I recognized anyway and didn't look at him much. It was Alicia who had always intrigued me. Just as you do now." He snapped off a bud and twirled it between his thumb and first finger. "And you have to admit, you and Henry were married very quickly considering his wife had recently perished in a mysterious carriage accident. How was it you two met?"

"It wasn't mysterious at all as I understand it. The driver lost control." She felt perspiration soak the back of her camisole and hoped it wouldn't show through onto the dress she wore. "Henry and I met through mutual friends. Henry needed a mother for the children, and I have always wanted children. We didn't wish to let too much time pass or the children would have suffered." She put the last of the flowers along with the greenery she planned to use into the basket and turned with the sharp point of the shears toward his vulnerable mid-section.

His eyes widened, and he stepped back giving her plenty of room to make the corner and head to the door. "Enjoy the flowers, Timothy. I'm sure the humidity will help sweat out those poisonous alcoholic humors from your body."

She kept the shearers with her rather than place them in the leather holder where they were usually kept and tried to keep her pace even as she went to the cutting room. Once there, she expelled a held breath and leaned against the high counter. What an odious man. How could he be part of this family? How had he turned out so badly while the rest were so charming? She shivered in disgust and tried to concentrate on the lovely flowers and how beautiful they would appear under the chandeliers' lights.

She heard the men return through the rear door with the stomping of feet and the jovial calls to one another about who found the biggest bunch of mistletoe or the most holly berries. Meeting them at the top of the steps, she found the noise had been made by her husband, Lucas, the younger male cousins, and two footmen holding branches of evergreens. The men were removing their thick fur lined gloves before unbuttoning their greatcoats.

"Oh, put everything down here to dry off. I can't work with wet greens." She held her skirt back so the footmen could descend to the cooler basement and looked at the red cheeks of the others. "Seems as if you are ready for the mulled wine and hot chocolate being served in the blue parlor. I think there will be ginger cake as well." This last had been meant for the boys in their teens, but the adult males smiled overhearing her words as well.

"The rest came in the front door so they could get rid of their coats. Enough for all of us is there?" Henry's eyes rested on her a moment longer before he turned to Lucas. "You go ahead, but save me some of that ginger cake before the boys eat it all."

Lucas agreed they shouldn't let the boys alone with any food for too long and followed them. Henry pulled her to him, snuggling her body against his. He smelled like Henry and crisp fresh air so she nuzzled into his chest gratefully.

"All right, let's have it. Grandmother and Great Aunt Gertrude at loggerheads?" he asked while stroking her back and kissing the top of her head.

"I don't know how to tell you because I don't want

this family time spoilt."

He leaned back so he could see her eyes. "It sounds as if it's more serious than a little contretemps between family members."

"It has to do with Timothy." She felt him stiffen as she said the name. "I don't want you to make a big deal of anything. He didn't say all that much and he didn't touch me. I think he had been trying to get me to tell him something he could use against you, maybe both of us." She pressed her cheek against his waistcoat again before saying, "He's simply obnoxious and since I held the flower shears toward him, he failed to make his point."

"He frightened you—I'll kill him."

She held onto her husband tightly. "No, I think that would please him, and also it would let him know how to upset you. I don't want him to have that power over you—over either of us."

"What am I to do then? Tell me everything he said." He continued to stroke her back as she told him Timothy's words and what she thought the man meant as well. Henry replied, "I can live with him knowing Alicia may have been unfaithful, but that is all. He best forget he ever knew what might have gone on, because if Mary or Michael ever gets hint of such a thing, I'll know where it came from."

"I think he wanted me to confirm his suspicions, but I didn't. Earlier Eleanor said he needs money and he might have thought to ask for some to buy his silence."

"You probably have it right." He stood holding her in the servants' cloakroom.

"Now go and get some food." She gave him a slight push toward the front of the house. "I'll send up more in case the younger boys have hollow legs again."

"I think you can depend on that. I shudder to think how much Michael is going to put away when he's their age. He seems hungry all the time, even now."

"You can afford it. That's what you're always telling me, anyway." She dodged a hand that came out to swat her buttocks and left laughing meeting the curious gazes of the busy kitchen staff as she entered the kitchen.

"Stevens, you're still here. I thought you had plans to be with friends." She went to stand next to the man sitting at the table cracking walnuts and placing their meat into a bowl.

"I had been and then decided my friends were all here, my lady. Besides, I might be needed." He shrugged and broke another shell between his palms with a loud crunch.

"You are always needed, and you are more than welcome to be part of the festivities. Make sure there is a place set at the table for you. I will expect you to take your meals with the rest of the family."

He nodded in agreement. "My lady, I'll come and make myself known to all as soon as I get enough of these nuts ready for Cook." That robust woman stirring a large pot on the stove glanced over at the half-filled bowl and nodded.

"I need to join the rest of the family as well." Picking up a tray of cut ginger cake squares and motioning Stevens to bring the larger tray of sandwiches, they pushed through the green door toward the noise of family members having a good time.

"That's the end of the wreaths, everyone. Now we can bask in the candle's glow and sit back and enjoy." Everyone took her at her word and sat down to enjoy the beauty of the greenery surrounding them. There were still a few pieces to place in other parts of the house like the estate office for Stevens' enjoyment and the library. Sarah added praise where it was due. "Bethany and Melissa, gluing sparkles onto those pinecones was pure genius. They add another color plus shimmer. I would never have thought to do such a thing."

"Oh, Cousin Sarah, it wasn't such a stretch. Besides, once we began adding sprinkles to one thing it simply led to others." Both girls smiled at one another. A new friendship made.

"I think I'll find those glittering little pieces all over my dresses. My maid has already commented," Grandmother Simpson said, but in a much friendlier voice than she usually used. Sarah thought the old lady secretly enjoyed decorating the house and herself.

Sarah picked up two of the bowls of decorations and took them to the rear of the house dropping one off in the library where she hoped the aromatic scent would infuse the air with the spirit of Christmas.

"I know who you are." The silky voice from the shadows said sinisterly.

Sarah froze and then turned toward the secluded corner of the room. "I know who you are, also, Lady Cavanaugh."

"No, I mean I know where I first saw you. I must be excused for not recognizing you right-off since I rarely note anyone not of the ton or elegantly dressed. When I first laid eyes on you—you were neither. You were on the arm of one of my sister's lovers. A man I knew she had a dalliance with during her first year here in London. She had gotten a little wild back then, but Father wouldn't listen. He thought the sun rose and set on his Little Darling."

Sarah knew they were alone in library, at least. That the woman's spiteful words wouldn't be overheard by someone who would repeat them. Sarah waited for what she knew would be coming.

"Some man she had her eye on again. Before she took up with that artist. Her art master she used to call him. Told me they posed for one another. I even visited the house she had selected for her rendezvous, but that was before she had moved in, of course. After all, I didn't wish to be seen entering such a place on my own. Whatever would people think?"

"I don't see that this is any of my business."

"No? The exhibit where I remembered seeing you was of a few landscapes and flowers done by my sister at least two years prior. I caught a few glances pass between Alicia and your husband. I wondered if they ended up with a private showing at another time?"

"I do not wish to speculate since it has no interest to me."

"It seems too coincidental to me. To find you married to Alicia's husband so soon after Alicia's death." The older woman slithered toward her. "And when exactly did your husband pass on?"

"I do not wish to speak of such a sad time. We are here to make new memories for this house and the children. Memories they can enjoy for years to come. So, if you'll excuse me, I need to see to the table service." Sarah made sure she was quicker to the door to forestall any other topics of conversation Althea may try.

Sarah still worried over the conversation. What if the woman said something to the others? Began asking about Richard's death and how it had occurred? Would Sarah be able to stand up to questions that may follow?

She continued to the steward's office. She set the decoration near the lamp so the light would glimmer off the pinecones as she heard someone enter the room. She turned, smiling. "Stevens, I..."

Her words stopped as she realized Timothy had been the one to enter.

A sneer crossed his face ending any sign of attractiveness she once thought he may have possessed. "Oh, dear, did I interrupt a tryst between you and your steward? May I be of service since he seems to be elsewhere and you seem to be in a mood for..."

"Do not say another word, Timothy. Turn around and leave, or I swear I will scream this house down. If more women had done so when you trapped them as you keep trapping me then you probably wouldn't be still trying these juvenile antics."

He stepped closer making sure her hands were empty before doing so. "All of us are family here, after all. None of them will carry tales, so what happens at family reunions stay within the family."

"Then you best remember, I am new to the family. I still adhere to my own standards, and that means keeping men like you away from decent folks. Let me pass, and I'll put down your poor judgement to the drink I can smell emanating off you."

"That's the second time you intimated that I am malodourous. I don't think you've been close enough to state such as fact. Allow me to bring you much closer so you can judge for yourself..." He stepped toward her again.

She snatched the sharp-pointed letter opener from the desk and held it like the sword it imitated. "I may not be able to kill you with this, but I think I could wield some damage before you got it away from me."

He lunged at her, a snarl in his voice. "You little tease. I know what you want."

She held the letter opener firmly, but it wasn't as sharp as she'd hoped merely rending the sleeve of his coat rather than cutting through the sturdy material and into his hide. She raised her knee and connected with his groin just as he was miraculously pulled off her.

Stevens' growl of rage followed as he threw the man against the paneled wall. "I never liked you, Timothy, and now I know why. It wasn't simply animals you liked to torture and torment. It was anyone you felt weaker than you." Her steward pulled his right hand back and punched the other man in the jaw making spittle and blood fly from Timothy's mouth. Then Stevens' other fist came up into the man's stomach with an "oof" emitted from Timothy as he slid down the wall to the floor.

Not taking his eyes off the man on the floor, Stevens asked, "Are you all right, my lady?" His breathing was labored, but she thought more from emotion rather than exertion although the punches she witnessed had a lot of power behind them.

"I, ah, I am, thank you. I don't know what I would have done without you." She knew her hair had become disarrayed and the lace torn from her neckline hanging down over one breast.

"Make your way for help. I'll stay here with this cur until Bates or a footman arrive."

She made her way up the servants' stairs to miss running into one of the family. She certainly didn't want to meet any of them and need to explain. She clung to the wall to keep herself upright and headed upstairs. She would order Aggie back down to send help to the steward's office. She opened her door and slipped inside without anyone seeing her. She didn't want the reunion spoiled. They had all worked so hard, and it wasn't fair one ill-bred man could bring it all crashing down.

"Sarah? I need help with these cuff buttons, and Jason is nowhere to be found." Henry stopped as he entered through the doorway which stood open between their rooms. "What happened?"

The trauma of the past half hour overcame her, and she sat on the stool in front of her mirror heavily. "I…I…Stevens needs help."

Her husband's brows came down. "What do you mean, Stevens needs help? Look at you, you seem to need help yourself. Why worry about Stevens?"

She could only shake her head as she tried to tuck the lace into the top of her dress as if that would make it better. "No, I am fine. Stevens needs help in his office."

He left her without his shirt buttons done or even putting on a coat. "I'll know the reason for your condition or someone's going to be dismissed."

Still shaking, Sarah tried to remove her dress as Aggie hurried in. "I just passed the master. Did you two have a row?" Her friend's mouth dropped open. "Did he do this? I'll poison him."

"No, Henry didn't do anything, and the one to poison would be that Timothy. He attacked me, and Stevens saved me but needs help to get rid of Timothy before others discover what a degenerate he is."

"I would have to stand in line to poison that man, I assure you. Not a maid's been safe from his hands and the things he says he'll do to them… Well, it makes a body wonder where he got his ideas from, it does." She pulled the dress over Sarah's head. "Let me get you a bath and clean that scum's touch off your body, my lady."

"I don't have time. Just get the dress I planned to wear tonight and allow me to go down and greet the family before dinner. I'm not sure if we'll need to come up with an excuse for why Timothy isn't there, but I don't think he'll be able to eat anything for a few days. Not anything he has to chew anyway."

Aggie put up Sarah's hair and tucked one of the sparkle encrusted cloth flowers into the side. Sarah had promised the two girls she would wear it when they gave her one as a gift. She didn't wish to disappoint them, not tonight when everything may be crashing down on her family reunion. Possibly the last time they would all be together.

As she descended, she met a few other of the ladies who were all atwitter about how nice the house appeared and how eager they were to show off their handiwork to the others. The men had been shooed out of the main rooms and had spent the day playing cards and in the billiard room. The smoking of cigars and the drinking of brandy may also have been on the agenda. Henry had teased her saying he knew how to entertain his male cousins.

On pins and needles, Sarah wondered what had gone on in the steward's office. How Henry had handled his anger because she was sure Henry would be angry and probably at more than one person. She wished there was a way to go and tell him how thankful she was for Stevens' intervention even if it meant Timothy losing a few teeth.

Grandmother Simpson came down with her sister-in-law arguing about which general was the more attractive during their come-out and ended up agreeing Benjamin Franklin was the most charming of the men representing the American colonies. This was a discussion only women of that age could participate in so the other ladies were left to themselves.

Eleanor came in followed by Bethany and Melissa who noticed the flower in Sarah's hair and smiled widely. They sat to one side and spoke in low voices glancing toward the doorway every few minutes. Then giggled when Terrance and Hugo entered, the male cousins about the girls' age. Oh, so the girls were going to test their flirting skills on their second and third cousins. Sarah wished she was so young and carefree again. Any age where she didn't have to face her husband after being the cause for his cousin being beaten in the family home during a family gathering.

The men finally joined the ladies, and Sarah's gaze searched the group hoping to catch Henry, but all she could see of her husband was the back of his head as he spoke with Lucas. That man's hard expression did not make Sarah feel any better. She thought she should at least find out what they had done with Timothy, who was caring for the man and his injuries.

Bates came to the door announcing dinner, and the ladies stood as the men put out their arms to escort them into the dining room. Formalities were not followed here, either, with husbands and wives walking in together regardless of their rank. It was always a noisy entrance with this large of group, and she noted that both Terrance and Hugo sat their female cousins appropriately. Possibly the mothers had intervened to make sure their children knew the proper procedure to be seated at a formal event.

The table, extended to its full length, didn't allow her to meet her husband's gaze as everyone admired the table setting and other decoration. Bates had one of the servants add the colorful flowers along the row of ivy down the center of the table interspersed with candelabra. The greenery was present on every surface as well as swags hanging from the curtain rods and over the mantel. White angels, red bows, and red cloth flowers sparkled in the candlelight. The men made much of the trimmings, and the ladies appeared gratified with their praise.

The first course was cream of clam soup. Sarah sipped the long-time favorite, but felt dismayed when her stomach seemed to clench as she swallowed. Peering around the table she found everyone else enjoying the soup. She leaned over to whisper to Eleanor who was on the other side of Lucas immediately to her right. "Eleanor, does the soup taste all right to you?"

Eleanor, who had just finished a sip, nodded, "It's very good. I must ask Cook for the recipe since I think she used sherry."

Lucas added his approval of her doing so, and Sarah decided her stomach was in knots over the problem between Henry and her. Not being able to explain what had happened was affecting everything she did. Would he understand how it had occurred? Had Timothy lied about what had happened? She certainly wouldn't put it past the unscrupulous cad.

Conversation took over with a mild hum around the table. Since the men had been hidden away most of the day, the ladies listened as every hand of cards and every game of billiards had been re-told so no one missed the excitement of the trouncing of opponents and the announcing of the winners.

Again, Sarah tried to catch her husband's attention to no avail when she realized Stevens wasn't at the table either. Had Henry dismissed the man? A man who had been loyal to the Hargrove estates for decades? A man who had saved her from who knows what? Timothy hadn't seemed as if he was going to stop at a kiss or a grope or whatever else he thought he could get away with in his cousin's home.

The meal was perfection according to those sitting around her as each course was presented. They all tasted flat to Sarah, probably due to her worry over the conversation she and Henry would be having that evening once they were alone.

Finally, she concentrated on being a good hostess to the men sitting beside her giving them a chance to tell her how they had won a hand without letting their opponents get one trick or how one had cleared the billiard table before another could do so. She remembered to smile, to chuckle, to laugh outright. She remembered how to behave to make the people around her comfortable, but in the back of her mind were two questions which needed answers. What had happened to Timothy, and where was Stevens?

The puddings were brought in all burning with the blue light of brandy to "oohs" and "ahs" from the group sitting around the table. Even this bow to tradition had not brought her husband's gaze toward her, and she tried not to show how his ignoring her hurt her feelings. She began feeling as if Henry blamed her for what had occurred, her and Stevens. Although tears were close to the surface, she didn't think any of the others could tell.

And Henry never even glanced at her to judge her feelings at all.

She led the women back to the blue parlor where a pianoforte had the place of honor. Since it was Christmas Eve, the plans for the family were to sing carols and perhaps read a story of the nativity. Eleanor said it had been a tradition from the past and said she knew Sarah wanted to keep the traditions alive.

Bethany started them off with Hugo turning the sheet music for her, and everyone sang the favorite tune. Eggnog was brought in, creamy and rich with nutmeg, along with the tea service. Even though everyone said they were full when they left the table, there was room for this traditional favorite. The men came in a few at a time, Lucas standing behind Eleanor touching her shoulder just below the back of the chair and joined into the singing as did all the others as they arrived.

Sarah's gaze moved toward the door every time it opened, but felt disappointed each time when someone besides her husband entered. Lucas took the book and began reading the story as everyone became quiet. No one said a word the whole time the story was being read, and no one entered or left the room. Eleanor ended the evening by saying a prayer of thankfulness for a happy healthy family and wishes for more of the same in the years to come. Everyone who held a cup raised it in salute to a chorus of, "Amen".

Still, no Henry.

Eleanor walked over to where Sarah stood. "I knew Timothy wouldn't last long. He never does."

Startled by this revelation Sarah stuttered, "Wh-what? What about Timothy?"

"Lucas said he up and went back to London saying

we were too mundane and boring for a bachelor. I guess since there were no young ladies he dared proposition, he went to hunt elsewhere."

"Ah, did anyone seem to think that odd? Not saying goodbye?"

"No, I think most of us were surprised he showed up at all. The last time I saw him at Grandmother Simpson's there had been a question as to where one of her antique jewelry pieces had gone. Timothy tried to insinuate her maid had taken it, but the woman had been in grandmother's employ for decades."

Sarah nodded wondering if Henry would find something of value missing here as well. "That must have been unpleasant for the woman involved."

Shrugging, Eleanor changed topics dismissing any thought of Timothy. "I hope the nursemaids were able to get the children settled down. Many of them know Father Christmas is supposed to bring them gifts tomorrow morning." Glancing at the mantel clock peeking out from the greenery, she altered her words. "Well, this morning, I guess. I plan on placing my children's gifts down here so I can watch as they open them."

"That sounds perfect. I'll do the same," Sarah answered almost automatically. "I usually see the children much more than I have these last few days. I hope no one is offended if I do so from now on. We have a lot of time between now and twelfth night."

Sarah lay awake for several hours, and still no sound from her husband's room. She knew Jason had folded the bed covers down as he did every evening even though Henry spent the night in her room. But there wasn't a dent in pillow or mattress to indicate Henry had even tried to rest there. The man had chosen to sleep elsewhere it seemed. Somewhere Sarah couldn't find him to ask all the questions building up in her mind.

With so much to do in the morning, she forced herself to sleep.

The next morning was a commotion of shrieking children, ripping paper, parents' laughter and all-around good cheer as the children, including those not yet adults, received their gifts. Most of the younger children received a stocking with an orange in the toe, a few pieces of candy and nuts, and a toy. The older children received a wrapped gift. Bethany and Melissa received hair combs set with pearls, and the young men received driving gloves just like their uncles wore when they took out their phaetons.

Melissa finished passing out the gifts from Sarah who had made sure there was a gift for everyone, and Grandmother Simpson had a collection of scent and embroidered lace hankies to last the year. Bethany gathered up the brightly colored ribbon used to tie the presents closed to reuse. She was the most pragmatic of the younger cousins, and Sarah would write to her later to see how she was doing in her first season. Warn her to take her time before committing herself to one man. She only wished someone had given her that same warning.

With that thought in her mind, she decided to allow each family some time alone and went upstairs to the nursery with Michael and Mary. Sarah hadn't realized how much she had missed the children, their welcoming smiles and hugs, their willingness to share whatever they were doing, their unconditional love. She finally left them when their supper came upstairs and she knew it was time to dress for dinner, although facing Henry and his hurtful attitude was more than she thought she could tolerate.

His room was silent while she dressed and even when she waited till the sound of the gong. He must have already dressed before she came up. So where was he now? She had decided at some point last night, she wasn't going to be ignored or accept the blame for Timothy's bad actions. She grabbed a shawl and went downstairs watching the last of her guests enter the dining room. She walked in right behind a male cousin and saw her husband, properly dressed and smiling as he helped his grandmother and great aunt to sit. Tonight, they flanked him, and he seemed to be happy for their company. None of them spared a glance to her end of the table.

Sarah felt like making a scene. She felt like shouting down the entire length of the table until Henry acknowledged her. Until he faced her and she confronted him with...with what? She wasn't sure what had happened after she had left the steward's office. In fact, she wasn't sure what had happened to Stevens.

She was gratified that everyone had dressed festively with many women wearing holly with berries in their hair or the sparkling cloth flowers Bethany and Melissa had given all the women. Sarah realized she was the only one not decked out with the yuletide mementos. Fretting about Henry had taken up too much of her time. If he wanted to speak with her, he knew where to find her. Acting as hostess for his family in his home.

She schooled her features not to show how angry and hurt Henry's treatment had caused her to feel. Gazing at the people in front of her, she knew they were Henry's family, but they were becoming her friends, some very dear to her already. No matter what came out of this reunion, she would be glad to have met these fine people. Glad that Mary and Michael would have them to lean on when there was strife in their lives.

She led the women from the table, but instead of going to the blue parlor she led them to the ballroom, a room they had previously used to make some of the wreaths and swags in. The large log in the oversized fireplace had been trimmed with ribbon as well as the two fat candles encircled with holly and berries. The ball of mistletoe hung from one of the chandeliers closest to the furniture brought in for the guests along with the pianoforte.

"Bethany, will you play for us? It needn't be seasonal, simply something you enjoy playing." Sarah knew the girl enjoyed playing, and within a moment Hugo stood behind her turning the pages of the sheet music the girl had selected. The next song Bethany must have known by heart since Hugo sat on the bench next to her gazing at her as only the young can—without guile or deceit.

The men came in all together, some carrying their glass of brandy jostling one another in good humor. They quieted listening to the music, and several men searched out their wives to share seats with them or stand next to them. When the selection ended, Bethany curtsied to the applause and gave up the bench to another. Surprisingly, Lucas sat down and played several songs without sheet music, and the rest of the family sang along.

Sarah had been aware of Henry near the wall by the double doors appearing morose, his mouth set in a frown deep in thought. He didn't applaud when Lucas finished nor did he glance up even when it had been stated it must be time to light the yule log and candles. Lucas did the honors of lighting the log with the help of the paraffin and pine cones beneath it. Then proclaimed it the first of such logs and that the piece left over shall begin next year's yule log. They all gave a cheer and swore it would have to be at Hargrove Court since they could all fit into it even if some of the younger ones married before then.

Nodding, Sarah agreed. After all, what else could she do? Even if she were no longer there, it didn't mean the reunion couldn't continue. The staff had done most of the work, and they would remain no matter who else left.

Footmen snuffed out some of the candles in the chandelier while Bethany and Melissa took a straw and lit the large yuletide candle. The group began singing Christmas carols again which went from one into another with barely a breath between.

Sarah would think of her options later, possibly wait until after Twelfth Night, if she could. If Henry would leave things as they were.

Boxing Day was honored with many of the servants working their normal jobs, but most took part of the afternoon or evening off to celebrate with co-workers. Sarah saw Henry give out the gifts she and Stevens had decided on for the house servants along with coins while the local tenants came up to the house for a holiday drink and gift of a wheel of cheese and salted fish to take home to their families.

The meals were served laid out on the breakfronts in the dining room, and the guests waited upon themselves. Sarah made sure meals were sent up to the nursery with special desserts for the several nursemaids taking care of the little ones.

Sarah had organized the older children right after

Christmas. Lucas had explained the tradition that all the cousins had participated in whenever they were together. They wrote their own play or took part of a popular one and acted it out for the adults. He remembered there had been a trunk of costumes in the attic and found it earlier hoping there were things worth using.

There needed to be a little help from the adults, but it would be kept to a minimum. This would be to show-case the younger generation's talents. Sarah called out, "Bethany, you and Melissa will be in charge of the costumes and helping the little ones participate. It should be a play for all of you. I have material and props you can use if you need them."

The girls already had their heads together making plans. Bethany offered, "I can sew quite well, and I'm confident we can make everyone feel part of the play. Hugo will help make the scenery."

Sarah finished, "I leave it up to you then, ladies. We will see what kind of thespians are in the family."

Hugo asked, "Thes…what?"

Laughing, Bethany said, "I'll explain it to you later."

Sarah found the quiet of the conservatory soothing. Not that the family was rowdy, but there was always someone already in the room when she entered or servants needing information. Even with Timothy's caddish behavior fresh in her mind, she found the flowers and plants peaceful. That was until the voice she had wished would vanish assaulted her once again.

"My sister and I both had attracted Henry's attention at our come-out. Alicia, for reasons I didn't understand at the time, had been practically throwing herself at the poor man. I mean, what was he supposed to do besides what he had? No man can withstand an assault like that."

Sarah wanted to put an end to these tête-à-têtes. "Lady Cavanaugh, I prefer you not discuss the children's mother where others may hear and repeat. I want them to remember her as a loving and caring mother. To mourn her loss."

"It's not as if I'm telling just anyone. I thought it would be of interest to you. That I would have been the countess if my sister hadn't practically shanghaied Henry out of my arms."

"I'm sure Lord Hargrove knew what he wanted at the time. You and your sister are both lovely, and I'm sure Lord Hargrove felt quite divided."

"I'm sure that options were taken from him once Alicia told him he was to be a father."

Sarah was done hearing about Alicia and her games which had tied Henry to her for so many years. "That is quite enough, Lady Cavanaugh. As I understand things, you became engaged to your Viscount soon after their wedding had been made public. Now let us not dig-up bad blood and old rumors. It does no one any good." Sarah began to walk from the room as quickly as she could without appearing as if the woman's words had chased her away. She must remember to always be surrounded by others whenever Lady Cavanaugh had her nails out.

The woman continued, her words stopping Sarah from moving. "Do you know where your husband is when he's not in his room? When you ask to see him and he isn't available? If you had asked my whereabouts, you would have found us both."

Sarah bit her lip to keep from shouting that Althea would have been the last woman her husband would go to for comfort. That Alicia's actions had almost killed both the men in Sarah's life. "I have no worry about my husband's whereabouts at any time."

The woman had seemed so sure of herself, but continued to fish for information. "So, you have given him his freedom as my sister had? I understand once she had procured the needed heir, they were no longer a couple. At least, when out of the public's eye."

Sarah continued to place the cut stems among the ferns and Baby's Breath. She wanted to hear everything on Althea's mind. Learn what the other woman was after. "I am not discussing my marriage with you or anyone else, for that matter."

"Because you have some sort of hold over Henry? Some reason he married you when he could have had his choice? When he could have come to me in his hour of need?"

"I cannot speak for my husband as to why he did as he did, and I certainly cannot speculate on why he did not seek you out. I would assume for the same reason he chose Alicia the first time."

The other lady's face turned puce, but before she could retaliate, Sarah turned and said, "I need to send the footmen in to carry these centerpieces into the dining room. Please enjoy the rest of your day."

"I will make you sorry you came between us, you little nobody."

A voice boomed from the doorway. "That will be enough out of you, Althea. I warned my grand-nephew away from both you and your sister, but the boy was besotted. He learned the truth for himself, but too late."

Sarah wasn't sure how much the older woman had heard but tried to find some way of smoothing everything over. It wasn't needed as Great Aunt

Gertrude continued. "Gel, you will stop interfering in this family's business, or I will know the reason why. Remember, I'm old enough to remember everything about you and your family—and the skeletons hidden in the closets. Your husband has been thought to have dove off the back of his horse into that ravine merely to keep from having to go home to you. You made a much better widow than you ever were as a wife."

Althea sputtered but found no words in response.

The duchess walked closer emphasizing each word with the thump of her cane on the flagstone floor. "Both you sisters have given more grief to this world than any other two woman of my acquaintance. I will not allow you to undermine the one good thing that has come out of all of the pain. I will not allow you to hurt Henry or his family any further. Do I make myself clear, Althea?"

"Yes, your grace. I meant no disrespect."

"Harrumph. We'll leave the idea of respect for another time. Althea, I feel your visit has gone on long enough. I'll let the others know you will be leaving this afternoon. Perhaps you can look up Timothy and see how he's doing."

"Timothy? He's poor as a church-mouse and hasn't even a chance of receiving a title."

Great Aunt Gertrude rolled her eyes. "I was speaking facetiously. I'm sure there's some poor man out there thinking he needs you for a wife. You've already missed Henry this time around."

Althea rushed from the room without another word. Sarah waited, fingering the flower stems knowing Great Aunt Gertrude had words for her as well. She hadn't handled Althea's threats very well. Not well enough for a countess.

In a softer voice, Sarah heard, "I know you have had much to contend with, Sarah, during this reunion. It's difficult keeping everything to yourself, but remember, we all love Henry and his children. We are strong enough to help you carry anything you need to carry—or bury. I may be old, but I still have the royal ears and can hold my own at court. You are not alone…" Then, with the swish of skirts and the thump of a cane, Sarah stood alone with her flowers again.

That night Sarah's mind returned to the still missing Stevens. While the two of them had been trying to find entertainments for the family, Sarah had asked Stevens to write out the phrases to be acted out for charades that would be age appropriate. She took out the box marked adult and handed them to Eleanor since Sarah hadn't been feeling her best. This problem between Henry and her needed to be settled so she could enjoy these last few days of their gathering.

The only rule being that no one could be on the same team as their spouse, so the two sides were divided up quickly while Lucas picked the first piece of paper, opened it, and silently read it. He refolded it and lay it on the table then intertwined his fingers in front of him as he bent over and lumbered forward a few feet swinging his arms back and forth then up and down.

"A man praying!" came from Uncle Reggie.

"Someone beseeching God?" asked Grandmother Simpson.

"No, no, why would a praying man lunge forward like that?" Great Aunt Gertrude added.

Then Lucas took one hand and waggled it behind him like a waving flag which had even Sarah laughing at his antics. What in the world had Stevens written on those slips of paper? After no one guessed correctly, Lucas stood up and opened the piece of paper. "Elephant." Then sat down with the expression of one who had won.

"Oh-h-h-h." Many people on both sides said. Eleanor unfolded her slip of paper as they all resettled onto the parlor furniture and chuckled. "Oh, dear," she murmured. "Here it goes."

She placed both hands just under her breasts pointing her elbows out to each side. Wagging them quickly, she went up on her toes and then bent low humming while hovering over the fresh flowers mixed in the greenery on the table. People watched in amazement although no guesses interrupted her performance. Finally, she stopped and opened the small sheet of paper and read aloud, "A bumblebee."

Amid much amusement and people saying, "We really should have guessed that one." The next person was urged to read their slip of paper. While at the same time Lucas called out that he had done a credible elephant for which he hadn't been given the proper acclaim. Everyone raised their hand to be the next player.

Laughing, Sarah rose to explain the adults must have been given the children's clues, but then shrugged. The adults seemed to be enjoying themselves and, after all, wasn't that what this reunion was all about? She waved goodbye to a laughing Eleanor as Uncle Reggie strutted around scratching at the carpet with his foot and flapping 'wings' as he tucked his hands into his armpits.

She checked in on the children who were busy drawing pictures and talking together. Mary greeted her at the door to keep Sarah from coming in any further. "No, no, Mama, you must not see what we are doing."

"I thought you might need help." She laughed as she tried to see what they were making, but Mary was adamant. "Papa had to leave, too. No one but us can see what we're doing."

"Your father was here?" She was surprised she hadn't realized where her husband had been during the afternoon.

"He sat and held Michael for a while then left. He said he wouldn't look at what we were drawing." Mary became very precise in her statement.

"I will come up to the nursery later, then. Bethany, if you need anything you know where to find me."

"Thank you, Cousin Sarah, I think we have everything under control."

Sarah left glad she had thought of putting the older children in charge of things. It took care of two groups she had worried over entertaining. They all seemed to be having fun and bonding, getting to know one another strongly. She went in search of her husband. It was time to talk.

Another night without sound or sight of Henry. Sarah brushed her hair roughly as Aggie entered. "Aggie, have you seen my husband?"

"No, my lady, not for a couple of days. Did you still wish to wear the green?"

"I haven't even heard Jason in the bedchamber." She tugged at a snarl before Aggie removed the brush from Sarah's hand and smoothed down the mistreated hair.

"Jason is doing double, no triple duty since some of the gentlemen didn't bring their valet, instead, giving them the holiday off."

"I know, but I thought I could catch him long enough to tell him I wanted to know when Henry was in his room. I need to speak with Henry and…never mind, I'll talk with him given time."

"Of course you shall, my lady. With so many guests it's a wonder you're not worn to skin and bones."

Her good humor restored by her down-to-earth maid, Sarah laughed. "I think all the good food and special desserts are doing just the opposite. I may have to let out a couple of my new gowns. I swear I can't get that corset tight enough any longer."

"You're fine just as you are, my lady. You needed a little more meat on your bones is all, and that fancy modiste didn't allow for any growing room."

Chuckling, Sarah said, "I'm not a child. I don't think women are supposed to have extra growing room like adding ruffles to skirts as someone grows taller." She stood up observing the hair style Aggie had finished with a light green ribbon. "That will do, Aggie, now the dress so I can see if I can catch Henry at breakfast."

Returning to her room after dinner, and a day of not being able to talk with her husband, Sarah found a pair of satin bedroom slippers embroidered with clear beads and seed pearls. She stroked them knowing who they were from. Gazing toward the door leading to her husband's room, she chewed her bottom lip wondering if she dared confront him in his den. She allowed Aggie to undress her and brush out her hair forming a loose braid off to the side so she could lay her head onto the pillow without the lump bothering her rest.

After Aggie left, Sarah sat on the edge of the opened bed, the pair of slippers in her hands. Making a decision, she stood and determinedly marched into her husband's room. She was surprised to find him sitting by a fire.

"Do I have you to thank for these?" She held up the

slippers while her bare toes dug into the thick carpet.

He stood wearing only his banyan and slippers but didn't approach her. "I meant to give them to you Christmas morning, but I wasn't sure you wouldn't throw them at me."

"Why would I do such a thing? They are lovely."

He shrugged. "I was afraid you were going to leave me after I let you down. I failed you."

She allowed her hands to drop to her side and stepped toward him then stopped. "How did you let me down? I almost ruined the entire reunion with how I handled Timothy's behavior."

He shook his head as if he couldn't believe what she had been saying. "I failed you for allowing that man inside our home. I knew what he was but hadn't wanted to admit it. I guess I was hoping the mean child had been left behind and a man I could recognize as a family member came in his place." He scrubbed fingers through his hair leaving it spiked. "I should have stayed with my first instinct which had been to send him on his way immediately."

She reached his side and touched his arm as she set the slippers onto his chair. "It was the same reason I ignored the warnings he wasn't a gentleman. I so wanted this reunion to be a time for everyone to reconnect with one another. Get to know the younger generation as well as their contemporaries. I think we have succeeded. All except for Timothy, and I feel that was my fault."

He pulled her to his side and wrapped his arms around her. "No, don't think that. No one missed him, and from what some family members told me they're breathing easier with his leaving. Of course, most think he left of his own volition and not at the urging by the fists of my steward."

She glanced up at his face. "Where is Stevens? Did you dismiss him?"

"Dis…are you mad? I gave him a bonus. He refused to allow anyone else see Timothy to London. I made sure Timothy's wounds were tended to and Stevens accompanied him to make sure Timothy didn't think he should return for anything he thought he may have forgotten."

"You mean like your grandmother's jewels."

"Oh, you heard about that, too? Yes, he is getting a reputation for picking-up heirlooms that don't belong to him. I was hoping… Oh, hell and damnation, the man's a complete wastrel and evil with it, as well. Stevens said he found Timothy attacking you and had to pull him off." She felt him tighten his arms around her then lessened the strength of his grip. "I wanted to kill Timothy, family member or not. I think that's why Stevens said he would escort Timothy out of Hargrove Court and stay to watch him in London to make sure he didn't return unbeknownst to us."

She laid her head against his chest listening to his strong heartbeats. "Do you think he would come back? I'm not worried about myself, but there are so many children here…"

"No, Stevens sent messages that Timothy is drinking and gambling too much but doesn't seem to want to repeat his visit with us. I saw the mess his face was in when I got to the stable. That's where Stevens had him dragged so family members wouldn't be alarmed."

"I'm glad. Not for Timothy's pain but… Oh, all right, at the time I was glad Stevens had come in when he had and that he took care of the problem. I wasn't sure

I had the strength to ward him off for very much longer." She rubbed her hand on his chest hair showing through the banyan's lapels.

"Am I forgiven?" he whispered into her hair.

"Forgiven? You don't need to be forgiven. I thought you were angry at me. Angry that I hadn't handled the situation properly, as a countess would have."

"The 'situation' as you call it was handled as it should have been. And I'm so proud of you, of how you brought the rest of the family together. How you set about them mingling and enjoying being with one another, even for you trying to include Timothy."

"I wanted to make you proud of me. Maybe that isn't such a generous spirit on my part."

"I am proud of you, more than I can ever say. You brought me something I hadn't realized I was missing— my family. I can never thank you enough." He leaned down and kissed her mouth. "Will you stay the night with me?"

She smiled beneath his lips. "I thought you'd never ask." He picked her up in his arms and swung her onto his open bed. Dropping her so that she bounced before he settled beside her minus his banyan, the proof that he desired her plainly evident. Not hiding where she gazed, she smiled and pulled him closer. "So, you missed me?"

"More than I can put into words. I have been so afraid you would leave—even with a houseful of guests. I wouldn't have blamed you, and I was already trying to figure out how to talk you back home to me—to us."

He didn't seem able to resist kissing her lips now that he had said his piece, told her of his worries. She accepted the apology readily although she didn't blame Henry for Timothy's actions. The man's a menace, and it was a shame he was part of this otherwise lovely family.

Henry stroked her side bringing his hands to her breasts which felt tender. She nudged his hand away, and he focused on other intimate areas which she responded to easily. It had been too long since she had been in his arms kissing his lips. She arched into him, and he took her urging for what it was, settling between her legs and entering her in a long, slow motion. Then he stayed without further movement.

"This feels so perfect—so right. I was so afraid I, we, were never going to be like this again," he whispered into her ear before kissing her there.

Again, she arched her hips impatiently into his and received the response she craved as he set the pace that brought her to an immediate climax. Henry tensed and held her closer for a few seconds longer before relaxing next to her.

He chuckled. "If I had any concerns about us before, I certainly harbor no illusions any longer. You missed me as much as I missed you."

Since she was occupying his bed, Sarah felt she could stay as long as she liked, and she hadn't felt like leaving him yet. In fact, she couldn't seem to get enough of him and lay there listening to his even breathing and the heartbeat against her ear. She drew circles on his chest, the fine hairs comforting in their masculinity. Her hands travelled lower to admire the other masculine parts and found that even in his sleep he responded to her touch. Stroking that very maleness that gave her such pleasure, it grew in size and strength.

He murmured and kissed the top of her head. Since he seemed awake, she continued with her ministrations and threw her leg over him, straddling his body feeling emboldened by the position of control. Encompassing his erection, a sigh escaped both of them. He wasn't as asleep as he had led her to think. Setting the pace this time, she controlled their orgasm and took her sweet time doing so. Having so much power was a form of intoxication, and it gave her the strongest release she had ever felt. She rested on top of him for a while and then slid to his side. Now she felt truly a part of him, finally an equal in the marriage.

Sarah woke as Henry wrapped around her spoon-fashion nudging her leg so she was intimately exposed to him. He slid in as he kissed her nape and behind her ear. "I didn't want you to leave me. Am I being too greedy?"

Enjoying their unusual joining she felt cherished, his arms about her pulling her close while feeling protected by his body. "No, not greedy. I think we both need extra proof we are going to be fine after this, after the guilt both of us felt for no reason."

"Hm-m-m-m, I love you so much."

All movement stopped as she held her breath. Had he meant that or was it something he thought she wanted to hear? Should she tell him how often she had wanted to tell him those words or let it pass as if she hadn't heard his confession. And had he meant them at all, or was it said in relief she wasn't leaving him over Timothy?

He brought her to an orgasm even though her mind raced, her thoughts in a jumble. Still, she responded to his body, his pleasuring.

He kissed her bare shoulder holding her body tightly to his as if she would leave now the lovemaking had met its conclusion. "Sarah, I'm sorry I said that. I mean, not that I said the words because it is how I feel, but I know we had an agreement. I don't expect anything more from you than you already give, but I'm tired of pretending that I don't feel more for you than gratitude."

"Gratitude?"

"For everything. You are an excellent mother for the children, my family like you better than they do me, I think, and you are so very, very passionate you take my breath away." He brushed his thumb over a bare nipple, and she moved displacing the digit.

Not having to look at him allowed her more chance for honesty than she might have had otherwise. "It was easier than I expected. To love the children came quickly, of course, since they are such lovable children. Your family are wonderful, and I am glad most of them were able to attend the reunion." She took a deep breath. "And although I have not much to compare the lovemaking to, I must agree it takes my breath away as well."

"Then all is well with us? You are staying with me—with the family?"

She rolled toward him and faced him. She felt it only fair. "Always. I love you, Henry, and have for months. You are a very lovable man, even if you don't believe me. You let your first wife make you feel less lovable than you are, less of a husband than I know you to be, less of a man which in my mind you are superb at being."

He kissed her mouth. "I don't think I need quite so much praise to know we belong together and not for the children's sake. I need you for my own heart's reasons. I hated feeling the way I have these past few days when I thought you were planning on leaving me."

"I never said anything of the kind. I worried you hated me for causing a fuss with your family all here."

Shaking his head, he kissed her soundly. "We will not argue this point again. Leave it that you are perfect for me."

She grimaced as his chest rubbed her breasts.

"Sarah, dearest, I haven't been in your bed every night, but could it be possible you're carrying my child?" He leaned back to see into her eyes as if searching for the truth.

Trying to calculate backward and realizing how much time had flown by these past few weeks, a smile spread across her face. "Oh, I hope so, darling, I hope so." Then hugged her husband as tears ran down her cheeks.

Twelfth Night would be the culmination for the reunion with most family members leaving on the sixth and seventh. Tonight, after a special early dinner, the children would put on their very secretive play. No adult other than the nursery maids had been allowed into the room used to cut and sew costumes and paint the scenery. Sarah knew the children were all excited to have been allowed full control and, other than donating a few bedsheets to the event, hadn't been able to garner any information. Even Mary, who usually was very vocal about what she did during the day at their nighttime visits, never let slip a word about the play. Sarah, like everyone else, would have to wait.

The adult family members sat in the chairs put out in rows facing several dressing screens lined up in front of them. The play was being held in the ballroom, and the adults were as excited as if it were the opening night at the theater. Henry sat next to Sarah and took her hand in his, kissing the back of her hand before laying it on his thigh. She sent him a soft peek through her lashes before turning toward the screens once again.

Bethany came out from behind the screen wearing a white robe made from a bedsheet with a sparkling halo on her shiny long hair and began to read from a scroll she had unrolled. Her first words were accompanied by the screens being pulled to the sides and the stage showing a faux stone wall with doors inserted into it. Melissa, wearing a blue robe and white shawl over her head rode in on a donkey pulled, literally, by Hugo. The animal was not happy about the slippery wood floor beneath its hooves.

This was evidently to be a re-enactment of the nativity. The adults tried to remember this was a solemn occasion and held back their mirth as much as possible. Sarah hoped the animal was house broken or they were going to be in for an aromatic event as well.

Hugo knocked on the first door and made his plea for a room, and the innkeeper shook their head sadly, saying, "There's no room here." Finally, the last door opened, and the couple, the mule now more cooperative after a carrot having been given to him, were told they could use the manger. The screen was pulled across the buildings while another was pulled to the side to expose a manger and piles of straw.

Sarah covered her smile with her free hand when 'Mary' turned away and returned with a wiggling Michael wrapped in another piece of sheet and placed him in the manager. His first instinct was to try to crawl out of it. Hugo took out a gingerbread man and handed it to the baby. Michael sat back sucking the head and crooning.

Hugo, as Joseph, said a piece about having a lovely son, and Melissa acted maternal trying to keep Michael from standing up in the manager or spreading the now slimy gingerbread man onto her robes.

Bethany told of how the angels spread the word, and then two shepherds wrangling one lamb stepped from behind the wall of inns. They smiled and waved to their parents who waved back chuckling, but held on to the lamb who bent to taste the straw on the floor. Several ducks waddled in as well following a line of bread crumbs dropped by the diligent shepherds.

Then the three magi came bearing gifts. Their robes were quite credible with gems and gold braid around their heads and beards with mustaches. Oh, dear, she thought she knew where the hair came from for those beards as she peered closer at the now shorter length hair on Bethany's head. Studying the magi again, Sarah recognized Grandmother Simpson's turban with additional feathers on one of the three boys. Each said a fairly elaborate speech, then placed a gold jewel encrusted box or chalice in front of the manger.

Michael tried to pick one up, but refused to let go of the half-eaten gingerbread man so was unsuccessful in his attempt. Sarah buried her face in her husband's sleeve unable to meet his gaze in case he was holding on to his composure better than she was. She felt him shake, so he wasn't going to be any help. Other family members were still trying to remain aloof to the comical side of the play since the children were still taking every word seriously.

Bethany finished her lines and rolled up the scroll to applause surpassing the members of the audience. Sarah glanced behind her to find most of the house staff and a couple of the stablemen present as well, probably there to oversee the animals.

Sarah stood along with the other family members in

a standing ovation, and the children took their bows and curtsies with Melissa showing Michael what to do. Then all havoc broke out when the donkey decided he'd had enough, braying loudly since his carrot was gone. Another came out of Hugo's pocket quickly, and one of the stable hands came and took the animal out the French styled doors to the garden. The sheep went, as well, bleating all the way. The ducks settled down in the hay to watch the humans then tucked their heads under their wings. Even though the chandeliers were brightly lit, the farm stock knew it was dark outside.

Refreshments had magically appeared and were disbursed to the now thirsty and hungry actors. There was much talk and praise while children explained their part in planning and executing the tableaus. How paint had been spilled, glue unstuck, and a myriad of difficulties to overcome for the final production to be placed in front of a critical audience.

Michael, still wearing some of the gingerbread and not much else, was taken by Mavis after a hearty kiss from his father and a kiss and hug from Sarah. She hated giving him up but knew he was getting overtired being awake so late. Mary, who had been one of the inn keepers, covered a yawn and agreed she wanted to go to sleep as well and followed the other younger children up. Bethany, Melissa, Hugo, and Terrance stayed up with the grown-ups basking in the compliments from grateful family members for allowing all of the children to participate.

Then the talk moved to past plays the now older cousins had put on. Ones which included jousts and sword play, dogs dressed as destriers, and sometimes ghosts using the much-maligned bed sheets. Evidently an item mandatory for a good performance of any play. Sarah sat back and listened as the other adults talked into the night. No one wanted to end the evening since they knew the next day many of them would begin their trip home. She hated to see them leave, too.

Henry helped Sarah out of her clothes. He kissed her neck and then each of the newly exposed areas happy she was in his home, in his arms. "You looked beautiful this evening, dearest, a special glow about you."

"Oh, Henry, save the compliments for when I'm fat with swollen feet. I've heard enough talk this past two weeks to know what I have to look forward to." Although it sounded as if she were worried, he could tell she was anxious for every change of her body. So was he. Simply knowing she carried his child made him think of her differently, made him more protective, more grateful.

"I will rub oil on your tummy and massage your feet and ankles every night."

She glared at him in mock horror. "My ankles will swell, too?"

"It won't matter a whit since I find you so attractive and am so besotted by you, nothing will turn me away." He was now kissing her belly where his child resided warm and safe.

She shrugged her nightgown away and climbed between the sheets waiting for him to finish his undressing. "Tonight was so very special, wasn't it? Everyone talking and remembering past times here together."

"I must thank you for thinking of it, dearest. If it's not too much trouble I would like to continue and make it a tradition, unless you think it will be too much trouble with you and the baby."

"I would do it all again. Mary and Michael have both benefited from meeting their cousins. They were so adorable today." He heard the pride and love in her voice.

"They were. I can see them growing in front of my eyes, and it scares me. What am I going to do when Mary has her first season or Michael goes off to school?"

"You will do what all parents do—worry. But they are both good children, kind and intelligent who know they are loved. I think we can depend on them to do what is best. I think they have had the best beginning a child could ever hope for."

He climbed naked onto the mattress pulling her close to his side. "Have I told you how much I love you and how lucky I feel to have run into you that day?"

"It is the only thing I don't regret about that day. I think selling that house and furnishings and adding it to Mary's dowry was the best solution. I certainly never wanted any of it."

He didn't want her to think of her late husband, never wanted to share her with another man—even a ghost. "Even though Mary will never know why, it should belong to her, and I won't keep it from her. She will be our daughter just as Michael will be our son and this new little one—ours."

"I am thankful for your generosity in sharing them with me." She snuggled into him, nuzzling her nose into his chest hair.

"It is I who should be grateful, and I am. You took on two motherless children, a man disillusioned with marriage, a family so distanced we wouldn't recognize one another if we passed on the street, and you made us all whole again. You are the epitome of what a wife should be and much more than my countess."

She gazed into his eyes as he bent and kissed her thoroughly. "A wife and mother. It's all I ever wanted to be."

He answered, "So be it."

A word about the author...

I have been reading as far back as I can remember. Works too advanced for an 8 year old, but that didn't stop me. I loved words. In 2015 I decided to put the stories I had dancing through my mind into my computer where I could read them whenever I wanted. I now have over 85 stories of varying lengths—mostly novels. My husband urged me to get them published—even told me it was on his bucket list. The Wild Rose Press was my choice to put those first stories into book form. The Sweetwater series of 8 stories put into 4 books was released in (2019-20). I am pleased to announce this is my 21st published book.